"Powerful, memorable [...] sleepy small-town No[...] skillfully drawn image[...] crop and Rosy and J[...] enormous depth to th[...] though, Louise Shivers is a born storyteller."

Dallas Morning News

"With the first paragraph of this stunning little book Louise Shivers pulls the reader into the world of ''bacca country.' . . . The tale begins quietly, but like a labor pain moves steadily and inexorably towards its overpowering climax. The author's gift for communicating setting, character and sheer tension is remarkable . . . a mesmerizing first novel . . . an absorbing tale of passion, jealousy, violence and tragedy. . . . The prose is Southern and musky, soft and sensuous, undeniably female."

Cleveland Plain Dealer

"A simple story told with a trim elegance . . . Gesture, innuendo, revealing asides, many of the reasons we feel that subtlety is one characteristic of a strong novelist, are all in abundance here, and Shivers already seems a writer of promise."

Virginia Quarterly Review

"Like a poem in the best sense; it cannot be paraphrased, each word is perfect and necessary. And so this isn't a regional book that relies on local color. Each long, deadly, radiant, fragrant, perfectly cured tobacco leaf; each household chore; each corpse . . . is there for perfect artistic purpose. This is a book about bodies and souls, about life, and our place here on earth."

Los Angeles Times

"With this absorbing first novel we meet an author richly endowed and sure of her way. She puts to her use an honest, accurate and selective eye, a dramatic sense very much alive, and best of all a sensitivity to the pull and charm and magnetism, even fatality, of human characters whom life has thrown together in their time and place."

Eudora Welty

"In her first novel, Louise Shivers has realized brilliantly a novelist's dream—a perfectly credible character who is both good and evil, terrible and lovable. Her name is Roxanna Walston, and she spins a story as strong as spider-silk. At its end any reader should be shaken by the experience and grateful for the invisible power of its author."

Reynolds Price

"It's a tale that's been told one way or another a thousand times before. But, oh my, the atmosphere that Mrs. Shivers . . . has given to this version of it; the sullen sultry mood of longing and loneliness, the sense of dread and excitement. . . . It's one of those rare cases of a writer producing an architecturally structured novel without sacrificing any of the story's poetry."

The New York Times

"The engrossing short novel by Louise Shivers is alternatingly romantic and realistic with a constant down-home flavor. In the beginning, it is as intriguing as a glimpse of a comely young woman with one shoe on and one shoe off. In the end, it could be an informal history of human destiny."

Erskine Caldwell

"Louise Shivers has been faithful in picturing a place and its people and therefore she has written an important book. If you want to know what poverty does to people, read this book. . . . If you want to see the wave of the future, read this book, because if the New Depression continues, more Americans will be sliding into misery than any of us care to think about. . . . If you like your truth sugarcoated, you'd better clear off."

Rita Mae Brown
Philadelphia Inquirer

Here to Get My Baby Out of Jail

Louise Shivers

FAWCETT CREST • NEW YORK

A Fawcett Crest Book
Published by Ballantine Books

Library of Congress Catalog Card Number: 82-18536

ISBN 0-449-20536-3

This edition published by arrangement with Random House, Inc.

Manufactured in the United States of America

First Ballantine Books Edition: May 1984
Second Printing: May 1984

*For Tom
and
to the
memory
of
Will
Shingleton
and
Wallace
Francis Reid*

Here to Get My Baby Out of Jail

One

Red-headed, jagged-faced Jack Ruffin, his long arms dangling by his side, walked into Tarborough one bleak-edged day near the end of last February this same year, 1937. He stepped up onto the wide porch of the funeral home as deliberately as a casket salesman. Strother, one of the porch regulars who blew smoke, rocked, and watched people go by, tilted back on his rockers and pulled at his felt hat as if he was speculating on the fellow's odd-fitting suit and the peeling cardboard suitcase he'd artfully slid into the bushes. As Strother reared back in the chair, I could almost see his mind working on the idea that the young man was a walk-away from a nearby CCC camp. The stranger was asking for Mr. Will.

Croaking as irritably as if he had been absorbed

in some work of vital importance, Strother said: "Ask inside. I don't work here."

The red-headed man looked too spirited to be making funeral arrangements, and too different from the folks in Tar County to be making burial-association payments. He walked inside then, out of my sight, but I expect Mr. Will took him right on into his office.

I'm Mr. Will's oldest girl, Roxanna. I never have told anybody, but I was sitting out behind the funeral home that day when Jack Ruffin walked up. I was waiting there in the car for my husband, Aaron, like he told me to, when I saw this man walking from the direction of the train station. Something about the color of his hair on that gray day and the way he walked gave me a strange feeling right from the first minute I saw him at a distance.

My daddy, Will Stanton, is known all over eastern North Carolina for having a soft heart. When his friends and kin-people can't think of what to do with their boys, they send them to Mr. Will for a job. There were three or four funeral-home boys living there then, sleeping upstairs. They'd take ambulance calls or help with the funerals. "Sitting around playing Setback," I'd heard my stepmother, Ruth, say. "That's all they do."

Daddy scared up the money right before the Depression to buy the old Yelverton place and turn it into the Stanton Funeral Home. "There's just two things for sure in Tar County: 'bacca brings money and people die," I'd heard him say many a time. Since Daddy didn't have a big crop of tobacco or a

2

warehouse, he'd decided that the next best thing for him to do was bury the dead.

Tarborough was a good, wide little town. Daddy always said that it was built around a creek named Contentnea and the Atlantic Coast Line Railroad. There were trees along the main street, real tall elms as old and lofty as the Confederate monument on top of the mound in Elmwood Cemetery. In the summers any little stir from the branches fanned the cured tobacco smell from the warehouses and sealed it over the center of town like a jar lid.

I loved the town and its rhythms and smells. When I was a little girl, I used to watch the men walking slowly back to their offices and seed stores after dinner in the middle of the day. The women usually took naps. I'd help my grandmother, Georgeanna, shell peas or butter beans for a while and then go lie down and pretend to go to sleep. I'd really push my nose up against the window screen and watch the colored girls that worked as maids saunter out one by one, pushing the wicker baby carriages. They'd settle onto the low brick walls at the street corners to show off the babies, roll their eyes at one another and talk in low voices like humming bees.

The funeral home was downtown in a big, rambling old house. There were really three front porches: a tall one in the middle with long white columns and one on each side where people sat. The upstairs was used purely for storage and as a place for the funeral-home boys to live.

I used to walk by on the sidewalk when I still lived in town with Georgeanna. I'd look up toward the windows with their closed shades, the little crocheted pulls flapping against the window sash. I always wondered what the boys did up there. Once I even slipped past the rockers while nobody was around and glanced over the rooms right quick. I ran my fingertips across a white shirt and put my palm flat onto the shiny cover of a *Front Page Detective*.

Daddy sent the stranger on up the stairs to stay in Neb's room. Neb was the youngest of the funeral-home boys and everybody's favorite. He was built as slight as a sparrow, and I loved to watch him walk. He moved along like somebody on a smoothly pedaled bicycle. The other funeral-home boys were too loud and smart-talking, but I liked to speak to Neb whenever I could. He'd look at me through those silky brown eyelashes and then stick his hands in his pockets and look down at his feet and blush. Sometimes I'd think about what it would be like if he'd come out to Cobb Swamp Bridge. I'd think about what we might say if we were to sit at the side of the bridge and dangle our feet in the water and watch limp leaves float down the creek. I'd even thought once or twice about touching his soft brown hair where it waved at the bottom of his neck. But I knew I wouldn't. I couldn't. I was a married woman with a baby. I knew better than even to catch his eye and start anything.

4

Later on, he told me about taking Jack upstairs that day.

"I got to the top of the stairs in no time," he said. "Your daddy had stuck a Co-Cola in Jack's hand and I kept trying to give him a Chesterfield. He was just *diff*erent than anybody I'd ever seen and for some reason you just wanted to do something for him. When we got up there I told him that nobody fooled to come up there but us. I opened the door to the room and sort of kicked the dirty clothes out of the way. I told him to make himself at home and to use any of the shaving things in the bathroom. And, Roxy"—he looked right at me when he was telling all this, his eyes still puzzled by all that had happened—"the room was in as big a mess as it always stayed. The sheets were all balled up and hanging off the side of the bed, but they were starched and ironed—we send them to the Chinaman's with the ambulance linen, you know. Well, I just stood there smiling over at that Jack, trying to figure him out. He propped hisself against the door a long time looking at the iron beds. Looking at the top of the chest of drawers that was covered with our stuff—combs, tie-clasps, cards and Co-Cola bottles full of cigarette butts. Standing there watching him look, I could see where under the beds dirty socks and dust balls had rolled together. After a bit he said, 'Go out there and look in the bushes and get my suitcase and guitar.'"

If my daddy had had any idea what all was going to happen, he would've sent Jack Ruffin back up the railroad tracks even if Jack did say he was his double first cousin's son.

It was about two weeks after I saw Jack come when the hearse bumped across the wooden Cobb Swamp Bridge and headed up the rutted dirt road toward me. I was at the farm, standing in the yard at the clothesline, hanging out the washing. Baby was playing with her spools in the kitchen. A cold March wind was blowing and my hands were red. Away across the bridge I saw it coming, Daddy's old hearse, the one he used for errands. I thought he was coming to see me, and I wished I'd combed my hair and had on something besides Aaron's old lumber jacket.

The hearse got to the crossroads and ground to a halt, the door slammed, and it drove away. Startled, I was standing there watching somebody come toward me. It was Jack. Cold as it was, he was bareheaded, and his coarse, red-streaked hair stood out in the wind. He walked straight up to me and reached for my hand. I stepped back, but he held on to my hand and said, "I'm Jack Ruffin."

I managed to pull my hand away, but I couldn't say a word.

Looking at me, seeing my confusion, he seemed to get enjoyment out of the situation. Little lines appeared around his eyes, and for the first time I noticed the streak down the side of his face that must have been some kind of birthmark. He stuck his hand in his jacket and got out a cigarette, cupped against the wind, lit it, rocked back on his feet, flashed a smile, and pushed the Chesterfield at me—right up in my face: "Draw?"

I jerked and waved his hand away and heard myself say in a whisper, "What do you want?"

"I'm sorry, Miz Walston, I thought you knew I was coming."

"All I know is you're somebody I've never seen before in my life," I said, but that wasn't true. I'd not only seen him that day he came, I'd been seeing him ever since in a dream. It was one reason I was so scared.

The clothes on the line snapped like a shot as they flapped in a sudden cold gust. I jumped. He stuck his fingers out like he was going to touch my mouth.

"Well, Miz Walston"—he said *Miz Walston* with a sound like the whine of a mandolin—"if your husband didn't tell you, I guess I will. I've come to help out."

Right at that minute my husband Aaron's Studebaker pulled into the yard. I hadn't heard it coming, or anything else for that matter.

He walked away from me then and headed toward Aaron's car. I backed into the house, almost falling over the washbench. They walked over to each other, greeted and shook hands. When I got into the kitchen, the tinny tick of the clock sounded like my heart beating outside my body. I picked up Baby out of the Kiddie Koop and settled her on my hip. Walking over to the window, I bent so I could see them. They walked around each other, eying each other like dogs do. Both of them were tall, long-legged, about the same height. Probably about the same age, too, a little older than me, twenty-one or twenty-two, maybe. Both of them stood with their hands in their pockets. The calves of their legs, pushing hard against the back of their pants legs, looked like men's legs look when they're straddling the rafters high up in the tobacco barns, hanging the heavy sticks loaded with tobacco.

While I watched, they started moving around in the chicken-scratched yard, walking and talking. Their motions were like some kind of slow dance. Then they hunkered down, making marks in the dirt with a sharp stick. They passed it back and forth. As I watched them, I thought about my dream again.

It was a dream I'd been having ever since Baby was born nearly two years ago.

I don't know if I'd really been completely asleep when I had it or in that little narrow place between sleeping and waking where everything is a shadow. But it was like I was standing in front of the window in the spare room, the one that looks out toward the railroad tracks. All of a sudden, I felt like the side window was watching me. I looked out and saw two people standing in the mist between me and the tobacco patch. At first I thought it was two men, then realized that one figure was my grandmother, Georgeanna, in her rusty black dress and tight head scarf. She was talking to a young man who stood tight-lipped. Georgeanna was using the stick she always carried to make some markings on the ground. She made sharp, deliberate marks, and the man seemed intent on her every motion and word. When the methodical planning was over, they smiled a satisfied smile at each other, like they had made some kind of settlement. Then they turned and smiled at me.

The first time I dreamed it, I wasn't too startled. I had thought many times in the four years since Georgeanna died that I had seen her. Then, after that day at the funeral home, I dreamed it again, and I saw the man was Jack Ruffin. Now that I stood looking at him right in my own yard, I didn't know what to think.

The tick of the kitchen clock made me know that I'd been standing at the window watching Aaron and Jack work a whole lot longer than I'd realized. I should've had dinner started long before now. Baby had squirmed out of my arms and was playing doodlebug on the drafty floor. As I took the bread tray down from its nail on the wall, I could still see them talking and working. It was the old well they were working at. It stood between the packhouse and the path to the barns. Aaron had been fussing about that well for a long time, and Daddy must have sent Jack Ruffin out to help him with it. While I sifted the flour for the biscuit dough, I could see their lips moving, but I couldn't tell what they were saying. I realized that even though they seemed to look alike in some ways, mostly they were entirely different. Aaron had the dark hair and solemn brown eyes that all of us folks in Tar County have. And he had the sloping chest and kind of bent look that some tall, dark men seem to have. Jack Ruffin, on the other hand, was as wiry and tight as a coiled bedspring. He had that red, blond, brown-streaked hair that I'd never seen anything like before. His

9

nose was sharp. His wide, thin-lipped mouth pulled back over large teeth in a sort of grin. His eyes, as gray as the day, had a strange cast to them, as if he was looking a little bit past whoever he was talking to. They were eyes that seemed to have a pressure behind them. As Aaron stood there talking to him, his feet planted firmly, I noticed that Jack Ruffin never stood still; he was always shifting from one foot to the other, kicking at a clod of dirt, fidgeting.

They worked out there for nearly another hour. I watched them as I slapped and kneaded the dough and while I fried the hard ham. With seemingly endless patience they tapped here, peered there. Finally they seemed to be satisfied, and I saw them head for the house. I felt myself getting hot even though the fire sucked at a sudden cold wind.

Ruffin, Ruffin.

I tried the strange man's name in my mouth, touching it with my tongue. It reminded me of the rough, rushing water under the bridge.

They didn't come into the house; they walked over to the shed and got into Aaron's old truck that he used to haul tobacco. Sailing off onto the road to town, Aaron hit the horn with the flat of his fist to get my attention. He motioned that he'd be back soon. I could just barely see the red head.

I sat at the kitchen table, listening to the tick of the clock and the scratching on the radio. By the time Aaron got back, dinner wasn't fit to eat. He didn't seem to care. He just sat down and cracked some pecans and ate them as he did every night in the winter. Then he started talking about how Jack

Ruffin was going to come out to see us Saturday night.

"Why don't you cook us up a chicken stew?"

"A chicken stew?" Taken aback, I said, "When did you get to know this Jack so good?"

"Aw, Roxy, we're just going to check on the well and then pick a few songs. He's going to bring his guitar."

I was as surprised as if he'd said let's get in the car and go to Chicago. Georgeanna's voice, like a spark inside me, chanted

> *Chicken-in-the-car-and-the-car-won't-go,*
> *That's the way you spell Chi-ca-go.*

"We hardly ever see a soul, and I didn't even know you knew him," I said.

"I talked with him a minute a week or two ago when I went into Pender's looking for a string for my mandolin. He had one in his suitcase that he let me have."

I thought right then about saying something to Aaron about how funny I felt about Jack Ruffin, but something in his tone of voice kept me from it.

Our farm was about ten miles outside of Tarborough on the old Raleigh road. In the winter Aaron just didn't seem to know what to do with himself. He didn't care a thing about sitting around in the house. With the frost on the plant bed making it look like a sleeping ghost he couldn't do much outside. Once he got started on weeding and plowing and transplanting, though, that's all I'd hear. It seemed to me that all he ever really thought about was the tobacco crop.

"You hold that tobacco leaf just like it's a dollar bill," I remember saying to him when we were at the packhouse last fall.

"You love it too, now," he said defensively. "You told me the first word you ever said was 'bacca."

I'd had to laugh. He was right. Georgeanna had written it in a little pink silk baby book:

Roxanna Stanton, only child of Grace and Will Stanton. First word: bacca.

And then she'd written a little verse:

> *Acca bacca*
> *Soda cracker*
> *Acca bacca Boo*
> *If your Daddy*
> *Chews tobacco*
> *Out goes you.*

But I didn't think about the crop all the time like Aaron seemed to. I'm twenty years old now. When I was sixteen, Georgeanna died. After the funeral I chopped the front of my hair off into bangs, changed my handwriting into a backward slant (my stepmother, Ruth, and all the other people I knew at Tar County School wrote with the perfect curves of the Palmer method) and got married to Aaron Earl Walston.

When I was six years old, three things happened

to me, too. A sore-eyed girl from Green Hill ran across the tracks to our house and threw a black railroad spike at me. The sharp, rusty end of it cut into my leg right above the knee. When I ran screaming into the house, as much in fear of the sharp-tongued girl as in pain, I ran right into the arms of my daddy, who had come home to tell me that my mother was dying. Grabbing some white rags and the zinc oxide ointment, he bandaged my leg and held me close. Then he took me to the little stucco hospital so that Mother could tell me good-bye. They told me later (when I was old enough to hear about female trouble) that she had been pushing to have a baby that struggled for three days and then died before the doctor tried to cut. By then my strong, happy mother was too weak to hold on to this world. I always think of her sitting on a summer day under the rose of Sharon bush, slapping at a bee that kept trying to get into the blossom she was holding. She used to pull me to her full, warm body and talk about how she was going to teach me to play the piano when I started to school. As it was, Daddy took me to school the first day after combing my hair so hard my ears hurt. Then, after he'd taken me to live with his mother, Georgeanna, he went off to Greene County to that business school named Whitset. I still have the scar from the railroad spike—a little long white place.

On the morning of the Saturday that Jack was supposed to come out for the first time, Aaron seemed restless. He was peering out of the kitchen window after we'd eaten breakfast. He put the radio on, and picking up his mandolin, he ran his fingers over the strings and then laid it back down.

Feeling brittle and tense and needing to keep busy, I decided to go into the bedroom and sew up the little hole in our crocheted bedspread where I'd seen Aaron's toe keep catching. The spread had been a wedding present four years before from Aaron's Aunt Patty. She had made it herself out of tobacco twine. I could imagine her sitting night after night, her fingers moving the hooked needle, at the Walston house at Haw Landing where she lived with her brother and her sister-in-law, Estelle, Aaron's mother. We'd named our baby Patty Estelle but we always called her Baby. Except for Estelle Walston, who called her *Es telle* like every syllable was nailed down.

While I was sitting there with my needle working and thinking about the two women, both spindly schoolteachers who kept everything in place, it struck me again how out of place Aaron's marrying me had been. The first time I ever saw him was at Georgeanna's funeral. They buried her at Cobb Swamp Church where she'd been a member when she was a little girl. That was the church Aaron's family went to. It was right near Haw Landing. I was standing out there after it was all over. The others had walked away. I was just standing there at the grave where they'd thrown the dirt in, not knowing what to do. Ruth and Daddy were expecting me to go live with them, but I didn't think I could stand to. I'd been at Georgeanna's nearly all my life. I just couldn't go live with Ruth. I don't know why, but she always made me feel kind of ashamed. And I couldn't stay at Georgeanna's by myself. I was too afraid.

I looked up and there was Aaron standing looking at me like he'd never seen anything like me in his life. I hadn't noticed him at first, I was so deep in myself. But I looked at him then, right into those clear brown-flecked eyes. And I thought, "This is what I'm going to do." I kept looking right into his puzzled eyes, and I let it start up between us.

That was the end of his family's plans for sending him off to agricultural school in Raleigh. By the fall we were married and settled on Walston land.

The sound of the radio brought me back, and I heard Aaron come up behind me. "What you doing?" He put his hands on my hips.

"Is Baby asleep?" I shot back, wondering why I was irritated. It wasn't like I was half as busy as I was in the summer when I had to cook for the hands, or that I minded lying down in the middle of the morning and raising my skirt and getting sticky and messed up; I liked for him to touch and stroke me. I guess it was because he seemed to be doing it just because he couldn't think of anything else to do. Only the night before when I lay puzzling and trying to sleep I'd felt so lonesome all of a sudden and reached over and bent my knees into him, wanting him to turn and hold me, but his muscles had jerked and he'd shrugged me off.

After he'd finished, he got up and I heard his belt buckle clank as he went back into the kitchen. I lay there with my eyes closed, feeling lonely. My thoughts were low like the dark, thick water at the bottom of a river.

I puzzle and puzzle trying to figure it all out. The day that I heard on the radio about the school-bus wreck I was starting to fry pork loin pieces. The train had hit that bus, and they were all dead: the rope-jumping Johnson girls and their stick-throwing brother who had waited that morning like every morning at the crossroads, clutching their brown paper sacks—the oranges with the holes cut in the tops; the six others from farms down the road where the bus stopped and gathered them in like a broody hen gathering her biddies. Dead. Dressed up in their little clothes, lying in those stiff coffins at the funeral home. The porch, lot, everywhere tight with people. Daddy, gentle and good to everybody, anytime, but always holding up at funerals, not able this time to hide tears running down the sides of his face—*Going where learning what on an orange bus bound for dirt.*

But in a week, voices picked up, washing and ironing went on. The same train pulled into the depot. Buses ran again. The little graves shrank in the ground, becoming low leaf molds. And one day the same gravedigger will dig a grave for Daddy, and someone will dig one for me, and when that time comes, when I'm dying, will I feel as puzzled as I do now, unstrung, unquieted, my heart like a grape stain with no wine made? It seems like the

grapes are in here squeezing, fermenting, but what
has happened to the wine? All I've had is the "play
like" wine at church. "Play like this grape juice is
wine," play like this wine is blood, drink this in
remembrance of—of—what am I playing like with
Aaron and the farm and the baby?

The radio announcer's voice boomed out, "This is
station WGTM—World's Greatest Tobacco Market."

I went on into the kitchen where Aaron sat by
the fire. "I wish the sun would come on out." He
was holding his mandolin in his hand as he spoke.
Sitting in the big wooden chair with the instrument
across his knees, he slid his fingers around the
curved sides. I watched him. He caressed the
tobacco-colored mandolin with the tips of his fingers, barely touching the wood. The words from
the song on the radio filled the room:

> Said a lady old and gray,
> I'm not in this town to stay;
> I'm just here to get my baby out of jail.

Standing up, I put my hands on my hips. "Aaron,
if you'll go ahead and kill the chicken, I'll put on the
pot." He didn't bother to answer me but went out
and picked up the axe and walked to the coop.
Watching from the window, I saw the hen flop
around the yard after he'd wrung her neck. No
matter how many times I see it, I'll never get used
to the way a chicken still jerks and jumps long after
the life has been wrung out of it. Finally, he took

the axe and chopped the head free. Then he brought the warm hen to me to scald. I picked and singed and cleaned her good. Nestled up inside of her was a cluster of little eggs that hadn't been laid yet.

While Baby jabbered and Aaron went into the bedroom to take a nap, I cooked. The windows steamed up and the little drops of moisture ran like tears down the glass panes.

I had decided that whatever it was Jack Ruffin was bringing into the house, at least it would be something that wasn't there now.

As I worked it was as if that strong old woman Georgeanna stood right beside me. My hands slapped at the bread tray, my fingers kneaded the dough with a stroking, a fondling, not too light, not too rough. The sifting of the flour made me think of powdering the baby's little fat bickie. The kneading was like touching my own breasts. The roughness of the tray, Georgeanna's own tray, wooden against my hands, made me think of her and her uneasy feeling about March.

"I don't know why," she'd say. "There's just something *about* March. I never can draw a deep breath until it's over. Every bad thing that's ever happened to me in my life happened to me in the month of March. It's like some great big black cloud that just hangs there."

She'd look down at the floor and shake her head and then get a fresh pinch of snuff out of her apron pocket. Holding the snuff under her lip, she'd shake her head and mumble, "The wind, it's sumpin' in the wind."

I'd grown up hearing her talk that way in March and seeing her hold herself stiff as if her bones knew something and were braced against it. On the very first day of April every year she would become a different person: light-stepped and proud.

Having that knowledge of her March fear made it even harder than it would have been on that March night when I was sixteen and the stroke of paralysis had slipped in like some lurking animal and got her. When Daddy and the doctor reached the house, the silence in the room was like cymbals in my head, for whatever had been there was so obviously gone, leaving only her light, long-limbed body.

Before Georgeanna died, this dark time of the year was when Daddy stopped by to see us the most. He'd swing into the driveway of her little house on the edge of town. Georgeanna would usually be piecing on a quilt with something serviceable like suit-samples that Mr. Applewhite had passed on to her from his store. My mind had wandered all day in the narrow schoolhouse, wandered by the dullness of the teachers and flown out the window.

I would hurry in when I saw the car parked in the driveway and grab a sweet potato, hot and juicy from the oven, munching on it like it was an ice-cream cone. I'd sit on the floor, my legs crossed under me, and listen. They'd tell stories about Rawhead and Bloody Bones coming down the railroad track, and babies born without arms. While they'd talk, the radio would be playing music in the background, music where mandolins trembled and high-pitched men's voices sang about prison and darling.

Six o'clock!

From the bedroom I could hear Aaron's breathing. Something about the sound made me know that he wasn't asleep, but was waiting just as I was.

I thought, "Here I am in my little thinking box and he's in there in his. Neither one of us has any idea what the other's thoughts are." It always seemed so strange to me that one person could never know what another one really thought. Ever. In this world.

I heard the sound of a truck pull into the yard. I knew it was Zeno the gravedigger's from the way the wooden side bodies shook. Jack Ruffin was driving it. His footsteps scuffed on the porch floor, and before I knew it he was coming through the door. Feeling lightheaded, I tried to act natural, smoothing the tablecloth. But he didn't pay any attention to me. He and Aaron fell right into talking about the things men always talk about. When he came to the table to eat, he was as polite as a preacher.

As I went over to the stove to get them some more cornbread, I let my eyes look at the dark-red hair growing down the back of his neck. His clothes kept catching my eye, too. They were no different from Aaron's, but they seemed to have air from a far-off place still clinging to them.

Later as we sat around the table and they were sopping up the last of the broth with pieces of the fried cornbread, Aaron asked Jack how he liked North Carolina.

"Nice place, real nice place."

For one steely second he looked right at me, that little glinty place in his eye piercing me.

Flustered, I jumped up and started pouring more tea.

He never did say a word directly to me or Baby that night, even about supper. He thanked Aaron.

They set to playing as soon as we finished. While they tuned up, I cleaned off the table and got the hot water out of the reservoir to wash the dishes.

They were good together; Aaron's mandolin and the guitar blended. It had been a long time since I had heard Aaron play, and I'd forgotten how much I liked it. He was a different person when he played. I liked that person. He looked like the clean-faced boy I'd seen at Georgeanna's funeral and married.

That tense feeling in my body slowly left as they sat on the straight chairs, tipped back and played on and on. They played the old songs, "The Butcher's Boy," "The Prisoner's Dream," "Since the Angel Took My Mother Away," "The Unfinished Rug," and last, the one Aaron used to play for me, "Beautiful, Beautiful Brown Eyes."

By the time twelve o'clock came, I was on the

couch with Baby asleep in my lap. I could tell by
their eyes as they finally stopped playing that they
were carried away to that place where music takes
you.

Two

After that first night it became a regular thing for Jack to come out every Saturday night. He and Aaron would pick and sing and hum after we'd eaten supper.

"Neb wanted to come?" Aaron asked one night.

Jack nodded yes as he tuned his guitar.

They passed a glance between them that seemed to say, "It could turn into a get-together real quick. Let's leave it like this."

Sometimes they'd play all evening without saying a word. The working of their fingers was smooth and cunning, the rhythm sliding in and out, their eyes far away. By twelve o'clock they'd seem satisfied.

I tried not to look at him so much. Not right at him, anyway. But it was hard. It was like trying not to look into a fireplace when a fire was crackling. He didn't look at me, though, not those first days. He didn't look right at me.

Aaron was acting like he'd known him all his life, talking to him all the time to beat the band. Soon Jack started coming out early on Saturday morning, and they'd go fishing, even though it was still cold. Later I'd scale and fry the fish they'd caught and serve it to them, hot and crusty. I'm sure they took a drink or two behind the packhouse sometimes. Estelle Walston, like so many women in Tar County, would've had a fit if she had seen a jar of anything stronger than scuppernong wine. But I could tell. I decided that men just know how to do secret things. I'd hear them laughing.

Sometimes the playing would start off at the barn and go on and on until I'd get tired of waiting at the house. I'd pick Baby up and go down there where they were. Even when they were at the house, sometimes I'd feel left out, so I'd cook a chocolate pie or something like that so they'd stop playing and talk to me a little. But they'd eat it, wipe their mouths, and go right back to playing. Sometimes I'd wonder if I picked up Baby and walked across the field to the train and got on it and went as far as it would carry me, how long it would be before they'd notice I was gone.

April came in, and I felt lighter, like walking outside from a closed room and seeing how big the sky looks. The dark things I'd been afraid of in

March seemed a little silly to me when I felt the beginning of the sweet spring air and saw the hint of the leaves. Surely, I told myself, it was good that Aaron had a friend to play music with and it wouldn't hurt me to be around somebody a little. Except for seeing Neb once in a while and talking to Callie a little bit, I never talked to anyone but Aaron anywhere near my own age. Callie is my half-sister.

You see, right after Daddy got back from going to Whitset when I was six, he married my mother's younger sister, Ruth. She wasn't anything like my mother. She was little and real pretty. She had just gotten back from Raleigh, where she had graduated from college. They got married, and then Daddy had a new house on Robert E. Lee Street. He'd talked to Georgeanna about it, and he packed my clothes and took me over there. Ruth started putting red ribbons in my hair and things like that. I felt funny and missed Georgeanna. I'd cry for her at night. One day Ruth sent me to the store for a loaf of bread, and I guess I got to daydreaming. I was carrying the bread home tucked up under my arm, and I guess I must have squeezed it, because the first thing I knew, there were slices all over the ground. I could have died. Since I didn't have a dime to buy another loaf, all I could do was go to the house and tell Ruth. She said, "Well, never mind. I'll get it myself." But she looked over at Gyp, the cook, and the two of them did their eyebrows up and I heard Ruth mumble something like *vague*. That night I begged Daddy to take me back to

Georgeanna's little house. He did. I loved the way her house smelled like snuff and lye soap. I loved the tall hollyhocks that grew around what she called the little garden house out back. But best of all I loved the days when we would go and sit at the station and watch the big black trains come in.

It wasn't long before Daddy had a new little girl anyway. When I was eight, Callie was born. They said she looked a lot like me, but I knew they were just saying that. She was the prettiest little black-headed girl, and she had real dark-brown slanted-down eyes like Daddy's. She was smart and quick like Ruth, not like me at all. By the time Raider was born two years later, something seemed to be going on all the time at the house on Robert E. Lee Street. Then Daddy got so busy with the Depression and the funeral home and all that I hardly ever saw him. But Callie was always doing things like going to the library or something in her starched dresses. I wore the straight dresses Georgeanna made for me out of flowered feed sacks. I'd sit in the swing on the front porch at Georgeanna's playing "Let the Cat Die" and see Callie and Raider walk by together. They had each other.

By April I was beginning to think I had imagined the look that Jack had given me the first time he came out. Why would he look at me like that, anyway? Compared to the girls that walked by the funeral home all the time in their high heels and swinging skirts, I was plain and too tall. I didn't even know how to stand. Since I had Baby I've felt like I smelled like diapers all the time, and my body was different with a little brown line down the middle of my stomach and stretch marks on my skin. It was almost like a joke to me now that I'd thought somehow that his coming to the farm had had something to do with me.

The middle of April came, and for some reason he didn't come out one Saturday. I could see Aaron keep watching the road all day, and after dark he would look up every time car lights flashed and watch until they were clean out of sight. Finally, after a long time with no sound but the hammer cracking walnuts against the brick, he said, "I'm going on to bed."

The stew I'd cooked lay cold and congealed in its dish on the table as I sat and looked at it and listened to the clock's tick.

The next day the Walston car pulled into the yard after church. We'd just finished dinner and Aaron was fixing to lie down awhile. We never had gone to church after Baby was born. I felt ill at ease there and Aaron didn't seem to care one way or the other.

Aaron's daddy, Mr. Tatie, called to us from the driver's seat, "We're fixing to ride over to Eureka to see Aunt Sally Anne. We thought some of y'all might want to ride by Tarborough with us." As he talked, I saw Estelle's eyes take in the pot of dried beans I'd cooked for dinner and look over at Aunt Patty and kind of slide her eyelashes.

Aaron said to me, "I b'lieve I'll just stay here— why don't you and Baby go on?"

It was decided that they'd stop by Daddy's house in town and leave us there.

After getting Baby ready, I went into the bedroom to slip on something right quick. I got out the soft, silky underskirt that Ruth had given me to get married in, and as I let it slide down over my body it clung to my breasts and waist like somebody's hand caressing me. The excitement of going into town for the afternoon rose up in my throat, and my fingers trembled as I tried to fasten the snaps on my good dress.

When I came back in the room where the family waited, I broke out in tense laughter. Baby had picked up Aaron's felt hat and put it on her own head in imitation of the bonnets that Aunt Patty and Estelle wore.

"Baby," we all laughed. "You look like a cat under a collard," said Aunt Patty.

I didn't say it, but that wasn't the only thing she reminded me of. Sitting there perched on the edge of the chair, impatient to go, gripping her little pocketbook and wearing a man's hat, she looked for all the world like Georgeanna.

When we got into the edge of Tarborough, I sat up on the edge of my seat and looked out: one big warehouse building after the other.

The men on the funeral-home porch used to say, "Well, the railroad may be the *backbone* of Tarbor', but 'bacca is the *body*." And then one of them would rattle off to the other about how 'bacca used to be called "the holy herb of the Indians," supposed to cause intoxication, raise spirits, ward off hunger and thirst and cure all known diseases. I'd heard a man on the radio say that millions of people used it right now to put a thin film of smoke between themselves and the reality of a harsh world. I never had smoked a cigarette myself, so I'd asked Daddy what that meant, and he'd said, "The world is still in a kind of fix, Roxy. Nearly everybody's smoking cigarettes these days, and the kind of 'bacca we have here in Tar County is bright leaf, the best kind for cigarettes."

In my mind I could hear the auctioneer's chant as we passed by the warehouses, "Give me a ten, a ten, a ten and a half, ten and a half, eleven, eleven, lemmen, lemmen, *eleven, sold American.*"

It seemed like to me there was a rhythm singing through it from start to finish. Plant, weed, crop, slap, tie, hand, loop, bend, reach, a ten-ten-ten. *Sold—sold American.*

When we turned off the main street onto Robert E. Lee Street, I felt a little funny like I always did when I came to the house. This was where Daddy's other family lived.

The house on Robert E. Lee Street had been built by a preacher who was an actor too. It had a wide white porch with what Ruth called a *porte-cochere* to park cars under. Inside it had French doors and a long sun room where Daddy stayed when he was at home.

Callie's room upstairs had long white organdy curtains that blew in the breeze from the long windows. You could stand in that room and hear the courthouse clock strike and watch the traffic go by on the street below—the ice wagon pulled by a friendly horse, the milk truck swinging and clanging, the cleaners picking up and returning the dry cleaning, the cars, they all went by. The washwoman's children bringing the woven basket of starched, ironed clothes smelling like sunshine would look up at Callie's windows and wave. I used to wonder what it would be like to live in a room like that.

As I walked up the steps, echoes of when I was little fluttered around my ears. Summer voices calling, "Wash your feet and go to bed. B-E-D—bedtime."

Standing on the back porch later, eating a piece of cake that Ruth had put in my hand, I looked out and saw that the back yard was just the same as it had been when I had stayed there. Callie pinched the big piece of chocolate off the end of my cake, followed my eyes to the yard and said, "The coffin boxes are about to get warped, Roxy."

It surprised me to see how much Callie had grown up since I'd seen her. She wasn't a bit like the little girl that used to play house in the coffin boxes. Daddy brought the thinwood packing crates to the house when Callie and Raider were little. I had played with them a few times, too. We had built a town, almost. Apartment houses, cottages, a zoo (using the family cats as the animals) and one time, a three-story apartment, like Callie'd read about in *My Weekly Reader*. It was simple. We punched and cut windows and doors in the light wood and trapdoors through the bottom. We drew furniture on the walls with crayons and added tin-can phones, flower pots full of chainyball blossoms and tins of penny candy from Applewhite's.

Then Georgeanna and Ruth had had some kind of falling-out, and I suddenly stopped being over there any.

"Do y'all ever play in them anymore, Callie?"

"No-o. Raider put an end to that when he took one to the top of the garage and tried to fly off. I can still hear Gyp now. She came swooping out the door hollering, 'Lordy mercy, Lordy mercy,' and waving her arms in the air as Raider sailed down. Daddy said he's going to have 'em hauled off as soon as he gets around to it. Raider plays marbles or ball all the time now, anyway."

Ruth called from the front porch, "Girls, here comes your daddy. We can go ride now."

We all piled into Daddy's big black car. He said, "I've got to stop by the funeral home a minute, then we'll go to the bakery and get some johnnycake and ride you on home, Roxy."

At the mention of stopping at the funeral home I started to have a low, stirred feeling. Callie must have noticed something about the look on my face because she said to me real soft, so no one else could hear, "Roxy, have you seen this Jack Ruffin?"

I didn't answer. I didn't want to talk about him. I just shook my head.

Since it was Sunday, I didn't know if there'd be anybody much at the funeral home. But when we pulled up into the driveway and stopped I saw that the winds, left over from March, seemed to have stirred up the street, bringing the men from town to settle onto the porch like ragged winter leaves blown out of a corner. Not only was Strother there in his usual seat, but Milo Batts, the tailor, was sitting in the end rocker, his pointy-toed Garfields flat on the floor.

Ruth looked at him and sniffed. "Every day he leaves the barber shop shaved and talcumed and smoothed. I believe he *drinks* his three meals a day now. Between that old whiskey and the talcum powder, he's beginning to look like one of the bodies in there."

We parked in the driveway. I kept wondering who we'd see. I watched Milo Batts, afraid to look up, as Daddy got out of the car. I was as fascinated with Milo as if he'd been a lizard.

He wasn't doing any talking, just staring at the street, first at the Chinaman's directly in front of him, then at the Briggs Hotel with its sagging balcony—he lived in a room there—and at Powell's barber shop. His straight eyes moved across to Pender's grocery, Sharpe's law office, his own tailor shop, past the vacant lot, back to the toes of his shoes on the porch of the funeral home.

Since the car windows were down, I could hear them mumbling. Strother, sounding like a brine-soaked croaker, said to Bass, the movie theater manager, who was always complaining, "Hell, can't you be pleased? You've been packing 'em in like sardines . . . and popcorn . . . whew!"

As Daddy went up on the porch, I could hear Milo Batts speak up as if there was no one else talking. "Who you got in there, Will?"

"Fate Renfroe—freight train hit him there in front of the Golden Weed."

"Tear him up much?"

"Bad, looked bad. I worked on him near 'bout all night. That boy Jack came in and helped me—just wanted to. He's good with his hands—cool about it, too; he was eating a Bit-O-Honey bar ten minutes after we quit."

The mention of Jack's name blew through me. So that's where Jack was last night, I thought.

"Going to keep him?"

"Can't—he'd be a natural, but you know I got too many boys here now, one trying to be a preacher . . ."

Strother interrupted the conversation by mumbling loudly: "Hope he don't decide to be a *missionary* like that fellow from Farmville—went to South America and shot hisself to death."

Daddy ignored Strother and continued his sentence: ". . . and then you know I promised to look after Neb." He sighed and moved his head back and forth. "That fella Jack can drive, too. Had Renfroe back here last night before I could swallow good. I don't have to fuss with him about the siren either. When he needs it, he uses it wide open, but he don't play with it like so many do."

"He's been hanging around here more than a month now—what you goin' to do about him?" Strother wanted to know.

"Wellll," Daddy said, "something will probably come along. Besides that, I believe Jack can look out for himself."

As if he'd heard his name mentioned, Jack came out on the porch. I don't know why my heart started jumping. He nodded to Milo Batts and then, coming up behind Strother, took both hands and got a grip on the man's shoulders, tilting his rocker backwards.

"Wha wha-wha in hell?"

"Jest Renfroe giving you a goodbye," Jack mock-leered at him.

Except for Milo Batts, this set the group in the rockers off—guffawing and knee-slapping. It didn't take much. They were always ready for a joke, especially a practical one. In a minute, Strother was even chuckling himself. Milo looked as if he would have if he could have without breaking something inside him. As it was, he just sat there looking like a glass snake that had swallowed something too big to get down.

I stiffened as Jack left the porch, but he acted as if he didn't even know we were there. As he set off down the street, Strother called to him, "Go on, you shaggy-headed rascal, go on—if you think you can get by the hotel without one of the girls grabbing hold of you—and buy Neb a big box of popcorn."

Then I saw Neb moving in behind Jack. I almost called out to him, but I knew I couldn't do that.

We left and stopped at the bakery and bought big round johnnycakes. But for some reason mine stuck in my throat. I gave it to Raider.

Later, the car was raising dust past Cobb Swamp Church, where Ruth would have loved to have stopped and looked at the tombstones but Daddy said "no," when Baby set up a fuss about the string of colored buttons she remembered at this late time having left back at the house. Her dangling legs windmilled like one of those plywood toys that you work with your hands.

Ruth was rambling on about the cemetery. ". . . Well, as soon as Ben Shackleford died after sitting in that chair and not speaking to a soul for five years, let alone getting up to pee, Bonnie Belle married Jim Bill Strother, and *he* died right straight."

Daddy said to the back seat, "Callie, do *something* in the way of settling that baby." We still had several country miles to go before reaching the farm, so Callie stared over at Raider to try to shame him into helping, but he was as deep into his radio personality as his mother was into her tombstones. "Who knows what evil *lurks*?" Lamont Cranston had taken over his brain.

I hadn't been paying much attention, my mind wondering where Neb and Jack were going and who they were going with and all.

Finally, though, I saw that Baby was driving everybody crazy, so I took her and settled her in my lap. She hiccupped and sniffled a few times and then nuzzled her fuzzy little self up against me and went to sleep. I lay my head back, and the sun slanted into the back window of the car. I felt the beginning of one of those rare feelings that sometimes came over me—a feeling like warm honey flowing upward through the comb of my spine and settling into a well at the base of my brain. The sensation was so pleasurable that I held very still, not even moving my eyes, because, just as it was impossible to make the feeling happen, the slightest body movement made it go away and there was no way to coax it back. The car moved on as the faces of Jack and Neb floated in a kind of whiteness before my eyes.

The spell was broken when Ruth said, "I wish we had stopped at the Terminal Drugstore and got me a little bottle of Capudine."

"Why the Terminal? What's the matter with Applewhite's?" Daddy asked.

"I'm ashamed to buy any more there this month, don't want Mr. Applewhite to think I drink it. I should have got some, though. When I don't have any, my nerves just stay all in pieces.

"Roxy"—she turned to the back seat—"I believe you could use a dose. You always look like you'd be afraid to say boo to a goose."

Raider fizzed up out of his trance like a Pepsi that had been shaken and opened too fast. "He-she-it! He-she-it!" he sputtered.

From the look that Daddy tossed him from the front seat it was probably just as well for him that the car was pulling into our yard. But Callie and I couldn't help it. We fell to laughing.

While Raider boosted Babby piggyback and went

outside to run around and chase chickens, I went into the kitchen to try to stay out of the way of Ruth's gaze. She perched on a chair in the front room where the men sat tilted back in their chairs, their long legs dangling. Aaron's gaze kept stealing out the window toward the fields where the young tobacco plants would be transplanted in a few weeks. He and Daddy had already walked outside twice to look over the fields, squatting down and running the dirt through their fingers.

I could just barely hear their voices from the front room as Daddy said to Aaron, "That Jack fellow seemed so handy that I thought he was probably the best one to send out to help you about the well."

"Ah, oh, yes. I appreciate you sending him on. Hadn't had a bit of trouble since."

Daddy said, "Yes, he's a right smart fellow. Don't have much to say, though. Reminds me of somebody, but I can't think who."

About the time I'd decided I'd better fix a little coffee and go on in there and sit, Callie came in through the screen door. She motioned me over to her and, putting her fingers over her lips, she whispered to me, "It happened to me, Roxy. It happened to me last week—I got the curse."

My face got hot as I felt the old feeling of shame wash over me. All the old sick feeling came back as I remembered the day I got what I called the dread.

I had lain under the pine tree on the little grassy

hill behind the garden at Georgeanna's, my hand
shading my eyes from the sun, my knee pulled up
against the pain and bent for balance. I looked
through and beyond the shine of the pine needles
and watched the clouds form big butterflies. My
back ached with a new pulling pain and I wanted to
lie flat against the ground. It eased me. What I had
thought of for many months had happened inside
me that morning. When I'd gotten up and seen the
first red stains on my step-ins, I'd thought, "Now
look what you've gone and done."

In some ways I'd wanted it to come on; I was
tired of being left out at school when the girls
talked about "the pip"—but something as old as the
earth I lay on told me that I'd never be the same
again, and worse, I'd have to tell somebody about it
and try to find out what to do and what to do it
with. Somehow I couldn't imagine telling Georgeanna with her kind of reserve, with her dry bones.
In a lot of ways she seemed like a man. As much as
I loved her, she wasn't my mother. Ruth wasn't my
mother either. I didn't know what to do.

Strange rags. Washed in the blood of the Lamb.
White sun streaming through the dandelions had
strained through Jesus' pimento-red heart in the
stained-glass window at the First Baptist Church.
Clots of unexplained blood on the floor of the
cloakroom at school after Maggie Crowder had
hurriedly left the class. (But Maggie Crowder was a
feared, foul-mouthed girl from Green Hill, and
maybe it *really* only happened to trash or for some

undefined shameful things that girls from Green
Hill did that called for punishment as severe as a
trail like little pieces of raw liver on the floor of the
long colorless hall at Tar County School with the
portraits of Robert E. Lee and Stonewall Jackson
looking on.)

The same feeling of shame came back the next
Saturday afternoon when Jack Ruffin drove up with
his guitar while Aaron was still at the barn, when
he walked right straight up to me, as I started
nervously saying, "Hello there, hello there, Jack,
Aaron'll be right . . ." He stuck his nicotined
fingers out and pressed them against my lips,
pushing the flesh against my teeth, and said,
laughing that laugh, "Who cut you on, who cut your
motor on?"

It was May and the rain had set in. When it rained
like that, Georgeanna always used to say that there
was probably a hurricane down around the Outer
Banks. Day after day it rained. Every day I could
see Aaron watching the fields where we'd set out
the little tobacco seedlings in April. Old Mama and
her son Jabbo had come up from the tenant house to
help. Aaron and Jabbo had already ridged and
plowed the fields and spread the guano. They'd
pulled the little plants that were about as high as
your hand out of the plant bed and put them into
open wooden crates. We'd all four gone along the
field, one of us punching a hole with a stick, another

one sticking the plant in, and then one of us watering. Drop in and water, drop in and water.

From the rain-streaked kitchen window I could see Aaron working out under the packhouse shed, stacking tobacco sticks. He'd glance out at the fields time after time. "Hope the little things don't drown," he'd mumble when he came in.

About four o'clock Jack caught me by surprise. He usually came in either real early in the morning and went off with Aaron, or about six o'clock, just in time for supper. With it dark and rainy like it was, I'd thought the afternoon would be a good time for me to get my bath while Baby was asleep. I'd just filled the big galvanized tub with scalding hot water from the reservoir and was pulling my dress off over my head when he flung the back door open and came right in. Thanking the Lord I wasn't completely stripped off, I jerked the dress back down over my underskirt and scrambled for my shoes and started stammering.

He came real close to me, hemming me in the corner, and stood like that for a minute, pressing his fingers hard against the little place in my top lip that divides it in two. Then, laughing, he pulled away and went out the door, heading down to the barns to find Aaron. I stood in the kitchen feeling faint and shaky.

Every once in a while during that rainy evening as I cooked supper, I couldn't help but curl up the end of my tongue and stick it in the little dent in my lip where his fingers had been, over and over. It seemed like I could taste the cigarette stain.

That night, Jack acted like he always did while they ate and played. Never even glanced at me. I decided that I must have imagined the word he'd whispered close to my ear right before he went out the door, *pretty*.

Later I heard Aaron talking to Jack while I was in the bedroom putting Baby in her little nightgown. "As late as it is—and you know the roads are muddy—you might as well spend the night."

I heard them walk up to the front of the house, heard the scrape of the sticking door to the spare room as Aaron forced it open. He said: "Go on in there and make yourself a pallet." Then he paused a minute. "I don't know why you don't just bring your things out here and stay," he said.

In the cold, damp closeness of the next morning my eyes opened slowly while everybody else was still asleep. They felt sticky and strange, as if little worms were lying across them right at the eyelids. The wicklight of the lamp seemed to have rings and halos around it. When I went to the porch to get the stovewood, the house seemed to be held in a circle of fog. The stovewood left splinters in my hands, so after the fire flared up from the toss of the kerosene, I sat down to pick the fine slivers out with a needle. As I waited for warmth with my robe tight around me and my hair falling lampblack over my shoulders, I heard a sound. It was as if a bird had flown by me and flapped its wings. I jerked up.

41

Was it Jack getting up from his pallet? Startled, I looked toward the spare room. But the kitchen was empty and still. Realizing then that the sound had to have come from inside my head, I sat back down on the low bench, twisting my hands into fists and clenching them tightly to my body. Scarcely breathing, I waited for another sound, an echo, but nothing came. Finally, the heat from the stove, scorching my robe and reddening my ankles, forced me up, and I left and went into the day.

While we were eating breakfast, Aaron said some more about Jack staying. "Bring your clothes and things on out here," he said. "You think I can't use some help?"

"Well, I could. I guess I could."

"Why don't you, then? I mean, if you're fed up with things there, you can come on out here."

"I could do that."

"Shoot, I could sure use some help."

"Well, I could help you get the crop out. It wouldn't be the first . . ."

I heard him telling Aaron: "I could do that, sure, till market time. I've a good mind to get Neb to bring my things out and not even go back, but I guess I'll . . ."

"Come on out here soon as it quits raining," Aaron said. "There'll be plenty to do then. Old Mama's Jabbo been having spells again."

Aaron turned to me for the first time. "Roxy," he said, "clean out that chifforobe in the spare room so Jack can put his things in it." He looked at Jack.

42

"She's just got sewing stuff in it now," he said. His voice sounded light, and as I got up and walked to the spare room, my throat felt strange. A little excited feeling was coming up from my bosom and working into my throat like fingers.

The spare room in the front of the house had been used to store things. Georgeanna's old quilt frame was in there. She'd left only one quilt when she died, the sturdy dark-squared Random Patch type made out of men's suit-samples held together with a scarlet cross-stitch. The squares looked like bricks. She'd always wanted to make a quilt in the Trip Around the World pattern, but we never did get to that.

Later, I tried to make the room look more like a bedroom by taking the quilt frame down and moving it to the packhouse to store. I found an old iron bedstead that some of the Walstons had thrown out, and Aaron set it up.

After Jack left that Sunday, we didn't hear anything from him for a while. At least, if Aaron heard anything he didn't mention it to me.

It was still raining the next Saturday when Daddy drove out from Tarborough. Callie and Raider came with him.

"I mean we have got ourselves a gully-washer," Daddy said as he thumped onto the porch and shook the rain off his big hat. "Town's about to float off," he told Aaron. "Strother and Bass are ill as hornets." He laughed and slapped Aaron across the shoulder.

I was hoping he'd say more about the funeral home. I wondered if Jack was still there, but nothing else was said. Daddy and Aaron took off to go down to Haw Landing to talk to Aaron's daddy about something. Mr. Tatie Walston was the farm agent for Haw County.

Callie and Raider stayed with me. Baby was tickled to have the company. She clapped her hands and sniffed at the vinegar while we made pully candy. As we stretched and pulled, I got Callie to talking about the funeral home. It seemed like I couldn't help asking her. "Do you and Raider go down there much?" I asked.

"Well," Callie said, "you know how they are at school—always teasing. You know: *How's business? Pretty dead, I reckon.* Stuff like that. And they're all the time asking us if we've ever seen anybody dead. You know how old that stuff gets. But Raider and me got to thinking about it and decided it was time we did see somebody dead. We've stopped by there a heap of times after school and slipped around back."

Raider piped up then, licking his hands and talking at the same time. "We didn't even get to have May Day this year," he said. "Rained out."

Ignoring him, I said: "I used to walk by, too, but I almost never did go in."

"Well, we go in," Callie said. "All over in there. We've even been in the boys' room upstairs when there's nobody there."

"I already had my costume right ready," Raider said. "Callie too. Mine was white long pants and a stovepipe hat. Hers had a hoop skirt."

"Will you hush, Raider. I'm trying to tell her about the day we went to see the burnt-up man."

"Let me tell it," Raider said. "Anyhow, the Maypole got ruined so we won't get to wear our costumes till the Tobacco Festival, I don't reckon."

"Hush up, Raider. I want to tell Roxy about that Jack Ruffin. You see, we heard at school last March that this man got burned up and that they had him down at the funeral home. We slipped in the back door without anybody seeing us. Then we moseyed back through the display room. You know, Roxy, all those rows of caskets, so cold-looking with lavender and pink satin linings. I don't mind going up in front where the piano is or the office, but those other rooms! Well, we edged up close to the embalming room, daring each other to go on. Finally we held on to each other and pushed open the door real fast. Oh, Roxy, it was like an icebox! And there was this little thing lying up on the table like a log out of a fireplace. I mean, we got away from there quick!"

"I mean quick," Raider echoed.

"We went flying up to the front part of the building. Then we stopped. Somebody was sitting on the stairs watching us. I don't know why we felt so guilty. It was like somebody had caught us going through the boys' room upstairs."

"I whipped out my jacks," Raider said.

"Yeah, you should have seen him, Roxy. He got

out those jacks and started throwing them around on the floor like his life depended on it. I stopped right dead in my tracks. I felt just like a broom propped up against the banister. I couldn't talk or move back, just stare. There was this man sitting there, Roxy. Somebody I'd never seen before. And I don't know what it was about him, but he sure wasn't like the other funeral-home boys. I just stood there looking at him, feeling like a dunce. His hair was real bright-red. I've never seen hair that color before. The first thing I thought of was that if I touched it, it would burn my hand."

"Tell her what he said, Callie," Raider urged.

"He said: 'Hey, you must be Mr. Will's girl.'

"I said I was his *littlest* girl, Roxy is his biggest girl. And he said: 'Who's Roxy?' He took a long draw on his cigarette when he said that. I told him that you were my half sister and that you were married and lived on this farm. He said: 'If she's any prettier than you are, she must be *real* pretty.' Roxy, I blushed—I couldn't believe I was standing there talking to a grown man like that."

My own cheeks felt hot there in the kitchen talking about Jack. I hadn't mentioned anything to Callie about him coming out to the farm. But I realized that the day she was talking about must have been right before he came the first time.

I didn't want to call any more attention to my thoughts, so I put the hardened white candy in a dish and started talking to Raider about May Day. Raider was still talking when Daddy and Aaron came back.

On Sunday night, Aaron and I went to bed early.

"Well, we might as well go on to bed," he said. "We'll need this rest when the time comes to chop and sucker. Soon as the sun ever comes back out, it'll really get to growing fast."

We lay there, and neither one of us could get to sleep. The night before still nagged at us. We'd sat—both of us pretending we weren't waiting for anybody. There hadn't been even a car passing by on the road.

As we lay staring at the ceiling, a whippoorwill started up. *Whip-poor-WILL! Whip-poor-WILL!*

"It's quit raining," Aaron said quietly.

Lying there, listening to the bird, I felt a little soundless wave of life come from Aaron's body. Slowly, his hand reached over and slid up under my gown to cup around my breast. Scarcely breathing, I felt my nipples cluster up under his palm. Soon he was over me, under me, in me. It was different for us somehow, some kind of tension urged us on.

He had hardly finished when we were startled by a sharp rap-rap on the outside door. Grabbing his pants and stumbling into them, Aaron went to the door in his undershirt. Bewildered, expecting the worst—only bad news travels country roads at night—he lit the lamp and unbolted the door.

It was Jack.

Jack and Neb stepped into the kitchen. The three men stood blinking at the sudden light. I had managed to pull my gown down and wrap up to my chin in my robe, but my bare toes stuck out and it seemed to me that the musky smell of lovemaking hung heavy in the room. And was it just me and Aaron? Something about the way Neb stood, bending into Jack, copying the way Jack held his cigarette, the way he rolled his sleeve, the way Neb's long, light eyelashes flickered over to Jack constantly made me suspect before I could stop myself from the wild thought that not only had they walked into the smells of me and Aaron but they'd brought something of that closed room upstairs in the funeral home, where they stayed together, here to us.

Neb left, and Jack took his suitcase and guitar into the spare room.

After the first strangeness, the days at the farm started falling into place like stacked cordwood.

Spring was happening faster than even a quick eye could follow. What was a gnarling of a bud one day was a crooked leaf the next. The getting used to each other, the glances, broke into the rituals of getting up early, eating meals together, closing the house for the night. The strange voice in the house jarred me. Even everyday words like "Pass me some more black pepper" seemed to have a meaning that I'd puzzle over.

The mules had to be cared for. The garden had to be chopped. There were always clothes to be washed and ironing to be done. Sometimes I'd feel my back was going to break in two while I was ironing Aaron's overalls. Having someone different in the house made it all seem easier, though. After supper every night Jack would sit in the kitchen for a while, and he and Aaron would swap stories. Then he'd go to bed in the spare room.

One morning after he'd been there about a week, I was in the bedroom pulling and jerking at the sheet on our bed, trying to make it go down smooth. In my head I suddenly heard George-anna's words to her friend Mr. Applewhite: *"You can tell how a girl feels about her marriage by the way she makes up her bed."*

The first few months after my wedding to Aaron, everything had seemed fine. Soon, though, there was an edge of irritation under everything. I was ashamed of that ragged discontent that came over me. I'd think: *You've got a good husband, a pretty house on a good farm. What else could you want?*

I tried to forget the feeling because I cared for Aaron, was grateful for him. At first I tried to lay the blame to the fact that I was going to have a baby and felt weak and wobbly. Later, after the excitement of the baby's birth, the terror, the out-of-control feeling of an animal tearing at my body, my surprised body, I had the comfort of the warm baby. After the newness, the awe, the wonder of looking down at the baby girl as she learned to crawl across the floor, sliding on one leg, scooting around like a bug, and looking up and laughing at her own cleverness, after that newness, the edginess grew.

The feeling of needing something else—something I didn't even know how to put a name to—would make me lie awake, propped up on my arm staring out into the night. In my mind I'd hear Ruth say: "A man that squeezes a dollar never squeezes his wife." Aaron squeezed me sometimes. Every Saturday night, right before we went to sleep, he'd lay out the little towel by the bed, and I'd know exactly what he was going to do. Sometimes I wished he'd let me hug him during the week, but generally he liked to do everything the same way at the same time. That's one reason I was surprised at him asking Jack to come out to the farm to stay.

Putting the last jerk to the bedspread, I glanced up toward the dresser. In the mirror I saw the reflection of Jack Ruffin standing by the front door. He had his cap in his hand. I guess he'd come in to get it. He was looking into the little oblong parlor mirror, watching me. For a round marble of time, we both stood, looking. As soon as I could, I pulled away, picked up the broom, swept to the back porch. Then I went into the back yard and started shooing the chickens around.

The spring days passed with work and looks and sounds. I woke up early, wide awake and eager, not exactly knowing why. Colors were brighter, everything was sharper. My step was quicker. I laughed easier. My body arched to Aaron at night, feeling muscular and tight like a boy's. Sometimes Jack

Ruffin would pass me in the hallway, and our hands would almost brush. Our eyes would meet each other's across the room. Whole mornings, afternoons would go by on just one look. Having him in the house made me feel prettier, brighter, quicker, smarter, faster. I felt that I had energy that had never been tried. The actual thought hadn't come yet—I hadn't put a name to it—just the high feeling.

Sometimes Jack would bend over me at the table, his mouth almost touching me. I felt seized, my mouth was wet, my knees went weak. I was starting to ache, ache to touch him, touch his face, his mouth. I could stand and look at his mouth and think: *Something is about to happen to me. It's getting closer and closer.* But we still kept words straight and commonplace.

Aaron had said from the first that Jack was to make himself at home and come and go as he pleased.

"You know where I keep the keys," he'd say. "If you need the truck, use it."

I don't know when I first started listening in the night from our room. Listening for the sound of the door opening in the night. I didn't even know that I was doing it. It was just out of curiosity, I thought, that I would look in the mornings to see if the truck was still parked in the same place or if it had moved in its tracks in the night; if the door latch had been left ajar; if there were any strange tracks in the yard.

One morning I did see tracks and, my throat feeling strange, I looked down at the markings, brushed them with my foot, imagining Neb coming in the dead of night to get Jack—I saw them laugh at some secret. Then, looking up into sunstreaks rainbowing through the chainyball trees, I realized my mind had imagined a whole scene just because I saw the big tire tracks of the ambulance up under the front window. In a flash I also saw a dark upstairs room in the funeral home where the only light came from the neon sign of the filling station out front. The light was blue like a milk-of-magnesia bottle, reflecting on Jack's bare leg, cutting through the smoke of his cigarette, finding the glossy covers of detective magazines and finally setting on Neb's trembling fingers. Under the bed, covered with dustballs, I saw the postcard that had stuck in my mind ever since the day so long ago when I snuck into the upstairs: the picture of the cut-off head of a cat and, in another place, the cat's cut-off tail and the block words: DON'T LOSE YOUR HEAD OVER A LITTLE PIECE OF TAIL.

I tried to shake off my sick feeling and not act funny at breakfast, but I found myself stiff and tense as I slapped the eggs on the plate. Jack didn't look at me at all as he did some mornings, but spoke to Aaron. "Neb came by last night."

"Uh-huh."

"Needed some help at a wreck down by Johnson Crossroads. Fellow riding with him took a rigor."

"Anybody hurt much?"

"An old preacher and his wife swerved in a ditch, both of them hurt pretty bad. I don't know what they were doing riding at that time a-night."

I felt the jealous pull relax. How could I have imagined such things! He was telling the truth, I knew. He'd just been working.

Aaron tapped his cigarette on the edge of the table. "You're bound to be half asleep," he said. "We don't have too much to chop today. Why don't you come up to the house and take a nap after dinner? I can finish up."

Jack nodded that he might do that.

They walked out together to the field, leaving me the whole morning to work and think on the day ahead.

On that green spring evening, I watched the cat walk across the yard toward the garden. Her sides were so swollen that she looked like a possum. I wondered if she hurt, if the pressure of carrying the kitten babies was the same for her on four legs as it had been for me on two. I remembered the feeling of strain inside the top of my thighs before Baby was born, a sluggish, sprung feeling. I looked down at Baby on the pallet on the kitchen floor. She was sprawled out on her stomach, sleeping. And I thought: *In the spare room, how is Jack Ruffin sleeping? Is he lying flat on his stomach?* I'd tried to get used to the idea of him living there, but that strange man lying asleep on the bed in the daytime made me uneasy. I kept trying to push the thought of him away. I would have felt strange if *any*body was staying there with us. I tried to settle into some kind of routine and keep my thoughts on what I was doing. The garden was planted and growing fast. The garden peas looked just like flowers. I remember feeling foolish and self-conscious as I bent to smell them. Restless. Not that he talked to me or looked at me, but I knew he was watching me every minute. As if he could see me sitting in a chair in the kitchen right through the wall. I heard the sound of his shoes hit the boards, and I jumped like a pullet. I thought: I ought to be doing something now instead of sitting here nailed to the chair. My breasts are little and my hand goes inside my dress to wonder about them. I've done this several times lately. This puzzles me. I wonder if he's lying facing me on the other side of that wall? Ruth says she believes I think too much. What is all this thinking going to lead me to?

Three

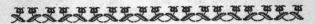

One Saturday in June, Aaron went to town to tend to some business and took Baby with him to see his folks. Jack had left earlier, saying he had some business in Raleigh. When Aaron started out the door, he called back to me, "I'm going to stay up there awhile. Your daddy and Ruth will probably want to bring Baby on back after a bit."

When they were gone I stood in the door and thought, "I need a few minutes by myself before Ruth is out here pushing at me."

Slamming the screen door, I decided that I was going to wash my hair before they brought Baby back. Out on the back porch where the stiff heat was teased by spirals of wind, I laid out my towel and soaps and the worn silver hairbrush and mirror that Georgeanna whispered I should keep. Ordinarily I kept them wrapped in chammy cloth in the paper-lined shelf of her trunk, but the new feeling that was on me today made me want to use them—to touch their cold metal with my face.

I took the band and hairpins from my hair and let it swing free. Aaron's words echoed: "Why in the world don't you get that hot hair cut off?" I hadn't answered.

Then I'd heard Ruth saying: "Roxy, my beauty operator would take you anytime and give you a new short style—you don't have to get a permanent, but my goodness, I just can't see why you want to wear it jerked up in a little knot on the top of your head." I hadn't answered.

Rainwater splashed out of the sides of the big basin, and although I'd sworn to myself that I wouldn't think about him, one of the water splotches on the porch floor was shaped like the soft brown birthmark on his face. I lifted a straight chair out into the flower garden and sat in the sun. Bending over with my head between my knees, I brushed hard with long, sweeping strokes and gave myself to the thoughts of him that reached into my brain like fingers.

The fingers pulled me back to another Saturday, one in May when the plants were still tender in the fields. He'd been standing on the back porch washing himself out of an enamel pan. Making up the bed in the back room where the window faced out onto the porch, I'd looked up and seen him. He jerked his undershirt off over his head like an impatient boy and slung it to the floor. The sheen of the hair growing down his torso in the shape of a tree trunk was brighter than the streaked red hair on his head.

I'd stopped fluffing the pillow in my hand. He soaped and washed his sloping chest and lean arms as unself-consciously as if he were at his own stream in some deep forest. He threw back his head as if to taste the spring air when he saw my watching face. For the first time we looked straight into each other's eyes. Slowly he began washing again, keeping my eyes. I could feel the smoothness of the washrag slide down his arm and then up the white underarm into the shocking nest of armpit. People moved around us in the house, but it was as if we were in a little box sealed with beeswax and couldn't stop the breath-holding communication until there was the loud sound of a pickup truck driving into the yard and Neb's voice calling out: *"Jack!"*

Now the hot summer sun that ripened the tobacco leaves to their gold dust dried the cocoon of my hair.

"Roxy . . ." I dropped my towel and the brush that was full of tangled black tufts of hair, and, of course, it was him standing there when I thought he was halfway to Raleigh. Him standing there feet apart, calves hard, eyes watching me.

Dear God, I must die from the sickness of wanting wanting.

"He gone into town?" Jack asked.

I must die, there is no way of holding back.

He took hold of my hand, and we moved to the shade of the shed. There was no thought of going inside the house or any other hiding place. The tobacco fields were fences. We lay down together in the fragrant dirt of the flower bed. Cotton clothes were no matter; an overflowing gourd dipper was tilted to the angle for him to drink. Our motions were like the unrollings of a Persian rug of many colors. Our tongues were the tenderest chameleons of spring. He put himself high up inside me as naturally as a silver shoehorn easing a silk slipper.

By the time Daddy's car pulled into the yard, Jack had gone down to the tobacco barns. I was bathed and lying across my bed, napping, with a whisper in my brain. The muslin robe that covered my body lay on me like broomstraw.

By the end of June the heat had settled over the county. The tobacco was ripe in the fields, and every week, every day, was centered around getting the leaves out of the fields at their peak before the sun burned away their brightness. "Burned up" were words that were always whispered in this part of the country because they could mean only two things: burned up in the fields because the harvesting wasn't done quickly enough, or the feared sight in the night of a wooden barn full of golden tobacco bursting into flames because someone sleeping there hadn't watched the stoked wood fires closely enough.

Helpers came out from town—maids, factory workers, children out of school for the summer, all glad to get the good pay and the change from town. Callie and Raider and sometimes Gyp came out to earn extra spending money. Daddy visited all over. He liked to see how each farm's crop was doing. He'd stay an hour at one place, then ride on to another, then back to the funeral home.

It seemed like Aaron's complete attention was on his crop. When the smell of curing tobacco from the first barn was in his nose, he walked around with a half smile on his face and whistled through his teeth. He worked every day until he was so tired all he could do was wash off and drop into the bed. Jack worked hard, too, in the fields, with the mules, but he seemed to save a part of himself.

When the "putting-in" started, Aaron and Jack alternated nights at the barn. Whichever one slept there slept in the big net-covered cot and kept the fire going and the barn temperature even. Whichever one slept there slept in snatches.

At first we'd just be together the nights when Aaron was at the barn. Without saying any words, Jack would take me into the spare room and do quiet things to me with his mouth. Once we started doing it, we just couldn't stop.

Barning tobacco was good, close, clean, hard work, with everybody doing his part. The men and mules in the field cropping and bringing the arrowhead-shaped leaves to the little sheds near the tobacco barns, the women and children waiting to take the leaves from the burlap-sided truck, to hand them in little bunches to the loopers, one on each side of the truck. The loopers slapped the leaves onto tobacco sticks that sat on wooden sawhorses, slapped and tied the harvested leaves onto the stick with cotton twine. A pattern and a relay from the field to the rafters of the barn established itself quickly, and hot day after hot day followed one after the other. The sound of summer voices, laughing, telling stories about hants and lost loves, passing the time as quick hands moved, filled the air and drifted on whatever stir of breeze passed by over Tar County, into the town.

But all of it rolled out in front of me like some kind of dream. I couldn't get enough of Jack.

All summer the radio in the kitchen played

I will pawn you my watch,
I will pawn you my chain,
I will pawn you my gold wedding ring,
Oh, warden, you know I want my baby out of jail.

In the daytime I was like a sleepwalker—walking slow, my blood thick as honey. I could hear the tobacco truck's wooden wheels rattling in the ruts coming out of the fields toward us at the barn. The tow-sack sides were high and the cropped leaves piled up. Here we stood working on the truck under the shed: Slap–hand–sling–twine–tie.

I looped on one frame horse and Gyp on the other, her black face shiny with sweat. Old Mama handed out the leaves, ready to take my place when I went to the house to start dinner.

Quiet as velvet, I could hear my own blood. I'd remember pulling his head down, groping in his hair, while his sun-cracked lips searched around the blanched thin skin to the earth color to the center— moving, tasting, drawing from the nipple the way to the well inside that holds water never hauled up in its own bucket before, but now moved even by the daydream of him.

Jerking up, my mind would come back, and I'd realize that the chicken was lying floured and unfried on the kitchen table while I'd been across the quilt in a trance. The field hands, Aaron, the children, all would be coming in for dinner in no time. My feet would light across the linoleum, moving with haste. By the time Raider, always the first, came bounding up the porch chanting *Roxanna, Georgeanna, ripe banana, Alabama*, the chicken would be fried, the cornbread sliding out of the oven, the tomatoes sliced and the butter beans dipped up.

I'd keep my eyes down as Jack washed, scrubbed the black tobacco gum from his hands. I'd keep busy pouring tea, glass after glass, for the thirsty workers, and I'd only nod when Jack would speak.

Pass me some more of those butter beans.

But I'd inhale his body from across the long table, know his dusty cured smell from all the others.

After everyone left to go back to the barns, I'd pick up the heavy workshirt he left behind—the one he wore for top cover at daybreak to go into the fields to crop the clammy leaves. I'd pick it up and burrow my face in it and inhale the wood-smoke smell of him until I'd realize I was moaning out loud. Baby'd start repeating my sounds. I'd look at her and listen to the strange imitations. Bird mocking a cat. My eyes would blur, and even when I'd reach to touch her, I'd realize that my own little baby seemed no more real to me than a picture in a catalogue.

By July I'd started slipping down to the barn. It seemed there was just no way we could get enough of each other. It was dangerous, terrible. Every chance we'd get we'd snatch at each other, slip, hide—and when we couldn't, it was hard not to be cross or surly. We'd stare across the kitchen at each other—our eyes dry and cagey. Watching. Waiting. I'd realized by then that the fond feeling I'd had for Aaron was just a weak hum compared to the raging thing in my chest now. I didn't think about the rest of my life. I didn't care. I had to have him. The way his eyes looked at me across the room told me he felt the same.

In July, the heat flattened out. When I wasn't going around in a trance, I was peevish. On the morning of the Fourth, Aaron started talking about going over to Haw Landing to a barbecue even before he'd gotten out of bed.

"The only reason I didn't go sit up with 'em to cook the pig last night was because that's one of my best barns curing out right now, and I wanted to see to it."

"Aaron, I just don't care a thing about going." The effort of saying that to him made me tremble slightly.

"Not go? I don't see why."

I knew he liked get-togethers with his family. They'd always been so close before he'd married me. Aunt Patty and Estelle had taught school together at Haw Plumbranch School ever since they were girls. When Mr. Tatie married Estelle, the three lived together at the old Walston place. And when Aaron was born, Estelle went right on back to teaching without missing a lick. I'd heard Aunt Patty tell about it many a time. "Aaron grew up at school as much as at the house," she'd say. The Walstons had always treated me well, but I knew it was a big disappointment to them when Aaron saw me at the funeral at Cobb Swamp Church and came dragging me home to marry instead of going off to State Agricultural College like they'd planned.

The bedroom clock ticked as loud as my heart. "I'm just not going. I feel like I'm in the way over there."

"Now, Roxy, you know they think a heap of you— and they love to see Baby."

"Aaron"—my voice was getting sharp and I couldn't seem to help it—"there's something about the Fourth of July that tears my nerves all to pieces. All the loud noise, firecrackers and all. Folks driving around in fast pickup trucks, drunk, having wrecks and getting their arms cut off turning over in ditches. It's too hot and everybody's crazy . . ."

By then my voice had built up to a pitch and I had started to sob.

He stood there looking at me. "Well, they're expecting us," he said. He pulled on his pants, and by the pants that he chose I could see that he was getting ready to go, and by the way that he tugged at them I saw that he still took it for granted that I was going with him.

"*No*," I said. The sound of the word in the room frightened me. It was shrill and high and brittle, and I realized that it was probably the first time I'd ever said it to anyone in my life, let alone Aaron.

He stood there blinking at me. His fine-boned face showed bewilderment. "Do what you please, then." I could already hear him telling his daddy, "You know how women get sometimes."

I lay across the bed for a while after he left, feeling sick and limp from the outburst. Slowly the sounds of the place came back to me: Baby clanking the spools against the side of the Kiddie Koop in the kitchen, the chickens fussing in the heat, the distant sound of Jack hammering at the barn. I got up and got a clean washrag and dipped it in the cool water bucket and held it against my eyes. Then I hung it up and got the shelled peas out of the icebox and put them in the big iron pot of Georgeanna's and started the fire under them. They'd be rolling in no time, hot as it was already. I walked back into the bedroom and sat down at the dresser.

I thought: "I don't believe I can stand to do another thing. I don't believe I can drag myself to." I sat down at the dresser looking at myself in the mirror, looking at my face, touching my mouth. I almost laughed. I kept seeing Jack's face so strongly all the time, a picture of it was so plainly before my eyes that when I looked at my own face in the mirror I saw his first, mine seeming to become his. I had to take my hands and put them on my own face and trace the features to make sure that it was the same face I'd always had and not the sharp face of Jack Ruffin, run my fingers down my own cheek to be sure that the long birthmark was not on my face but was still on his. What was the matter with me? Was I crazy? I opened my right hand and looked into the palm, at the little lines in it. I could hear Georgeanna's voice as she read my palm and started to tell my fortune: "Long life line, a long crooked double love line"—she would shake her head—"and the line of the mind, the line of the mind . . ." She always stopped there and looked puzzled. The line of the mind was long and at the end of it there was a big star. I never could get her to tell me about that.

I didn't hear the steps, didn't hear the screen

door, knew that Baby gurgled as she played but didn't really hear her, only knew he was in the room when I saw his real face bolder than the imagined one in the mirror behind me.

I turned willingly to him, my back straight, wanting only my mouth inside the hardness of his. I would do anything he wanted just to have that mouth close over me and take me out of myself into him. His hard lips first, then slowly, like torture, his tongue. What he did to my body was for him to decide, there on the couch with Baby in the kitchen in the Kiddie Koop, that was for him, that was the price I paid to get his mouth and the feeling of release that went to my brain.

"Oh, Lord," I thought over and over again. "What is going to become of me?"

Later, as he was standing by the back door running his fingers over the screen, he said, "I've got you a present." He turned to me and grinned.

I was dizzy. "What? Wait a minute. I got to change Baby. Her diaper's so wet it's about to fall off her. Hanging right down to the floor." As I made the motions to lift her out of the playpen, with her making little cooing noises at me and reaching her moist hand up to touch the wisps of hair that hung around my face, he went outside and came back in with something in a paper sack. After laying her across the brown couch to fix her and playing piggy with her little toes to make her laugh, I gave her her wooden Jumping Jack and let her toddle around in the room.

"Here." He pushed the package into my hand. Opening it, I stared at the small black rectangle, not saying anything.

"It's a Kodak."

"It sure looks nice," I said. I'd always thought I would like to have one for myself. Just for myself without having to ask to use somebody else's if I wanted to take pictures of Baby or a bird in a tree or just things that other people would think were silly if I used their camera to take.

"Come on out back, and I'll teach you how to use it."

We went into the back yard, and he showed me how to pull the little trigger with my finger. I had watched him put the film inside and stretch it and wind it, so I'd know how next time.

He went and stood in front of the packhouse and faced into the sun and said, "Now," and I snapped one of him. I laughed, starting to get the hang of it, and said, "Go get Baby and hold her up." He did, and my fingers were a little shaky, but when they were both smiling I snapped just as Jack called out, "Don't fold your finger over the little window." We laughed. Baby laughed too. We put her down, and she toddled off to look for her Jumping Jack, calling, "Dak, Dak." I guess she probably wanted to take a picture of him dangling from his little perch.

Jack said, "Now we'll try a trick." He went onto the porch and got some tobacco twine and did some things to the Kodak, then sat it on a chair he'd brought from the porch and called, "Come here."

67

He grabbed me in his arms and pulled me to him in front of where he had the Kodak sitting. Little aftershocks of our lovemaking went through me. He was kissing me and putting his hands on me, and we were laughing. He was whispering in my ear, "This is going to be some picture."

Then we heard the sound. A crash, a slouch, then a cry going into the dusty air like the cry of a strange animal in the familiar yard. We rushed to find Baby lying on the floor with the pot of hot peas knocked off and spewed out across her legs.

The night after we were back from the hospital and I had Baby settled down in our big white bed, I looked over at the lamp sitting on the dresser and thought, "This is the way this whole day has been, little beams of light going out in all different directions, shooting out in all different ways, none of them seeming to have anything to do with the other."

From the minute I had grabbed Baby up from the floor, reaching frantically for a clean sheet and diapers to wrap her in, and Jack and I'd jumped into the pickup and sped to the little stucco hospital across the street from where Georgeanna and I used to live, everything was a white blur to me. A white piece of the day. Jack left me at the hospital door, and as I'd stood in the hall, reaching for a big phone on the wall to call Aaron, I could see Georgeanna's house out the window, standing empty and still. Aaron was there in no time, and when he came in, I started crying, but I could see he was looking at me in a strange, stunned way. When Dr. Best finally came out and told me I could take Baby in my arms—she was asleep, worn out from sobbing, making little hic-cupy noises—I bent my arms like a stretcher and held her to me carefully. He said, "Take her on home and keep her in the bed and quiet. If she wakes up tonight give her some more of this. I'll be out to look at her in the morning." He turned to Aaron. "She'll probably be all right if it doesn't get infected. There'll be scars, though, bad ones for the rest of her life."

Aaron didn't say a word as we rode home, and I didn't see Jack again until he came up to the house to look at Baby. I said quickly, while Aaron was out on the porch, "Where's the Kodak?"

"I hid it," he said quickly, his mouth tight.

I felt so bad from guilt and pain for Baby that I couldn't imagine ever having any other feeling again. I wondered if this was something like what a man felt when he heard his woman screaming and being torn while she was having a baby. I didn't care then about the pictures or anything else; I just didn't want Aaron to see the Kodak and realize that Jack had been at the house when Baby had been burned.

Mr. Tatie rode up just as Aaron came inside to start getting ready for bed. The kind man called out, "Thought maybe you and Baby might want some barbecue, Roxy."

I knew that he meant well, that he was bringing the barbecue the way people would have brought flowers to a hospital room, but the sight of it when he took the clean dish towel from over it, the sight of the pieces of brown pork skin brought back the sight and smell of the boiling peas on Baby's tender skin. I grabbed the dish towel and ran out, out past the chainyball tree into the garden, spewing out a sour stream onto the sweet peas.

Later I woke up in the middle of the night. At first I thought it was the mosquito zizzing around my head that had awakened me. Then a rush of what had happened came to me, and I sat up in bed. Aaron wasn't beside me. I threw the sheet back off my feet and sprang over to the crib. Baby wasn't in it. I went into the kitchen. It was dark, and the back door was open. Through the screen I could see the glow of a cigarette from the porch steps. When I went out, Aaron was sitting on the steps, his thin knees sticking up like a bent knife in the dark.

"Where . . ." I started to ask.

He looked up at me, and even in the dimness I could see the accusing look I'd been expecting on his face. A thrill of fear ran down me, making me pull my gown close around me.

"Can't you take care of your family?" His voice was strong and bitter in the night.

"Aaron, I . . ." My voice was scared and embarrassed.

I saw then that he had Baby lying on a bunch of pillows on the step below him. As he talked he stroked her cheek and pushed back her moist wisps of hair.

"Let me take her," I said, almost begging.

He shook his head, a tight shake, stubborn and mean. "What kind of woman are you, Roxy?"

How could I answer that?

He wouldn't let me take her, and he wouldn't say any more to me. Finally I crept back and got into the bed. About daylight I finally got to sleep.

Four

$\mathcal{T}$*he tobacco* kept on ripening. The putting-in went on. I didn't go down to the barn for several days. I stayed at the house, keeping Baby as quiet as I could, keeping quiet myself, feeling blank and sick. Every night I'd think that Aaron was going to say something accusing to me, but every night he came in tired and dirty and went to bed as quickly as he possibly could. Jack stayed at the barn.

One morning at the end of the week, Callie slipped up to the house and came right out and asked me why everybody was acting so funny. "It's no fun at the barn, Roxy. We're about to get sick of the whole thing. If I wasn't planning on buying that dress at the Mother and Daughter store I believe I'd just go home."

I didn't know what to say to her. I didn't even try to answer.

I swore to myself every night and every day that I wasn't going to have anything more to do with Jack Ruffin. I was sure the spell he had me under was broken. I wasn't going to do a thing for the rest of my life but be a good wife. If I got too lonesome, I'd just have to stay that way. I kept as busy as I could, cooking and doctoring Baby's sores.

I often wonder what would have happened if Jack had left Tar County right then, if I had tried to make him go.

But after about two weeks like that, just cook, eat and sleep, I started finding it harder and harder to ignore Jack's eyes when he came in to eat, or to have him ignore mine. A little vein in my neck would start throbbing when he walked through the kitchen, but I stayed out of his way and didn't let it be possible for us to be alone for a second, and he stayed out of mine. No music, no joking around while they came in from the fields. Aaron kept a cold back turned to me every night, and in the daytime every time I spoke to him, he'd answer with a loud "What?" that didn't encourage me to say anything else. At night while he'd put up the mules, I'd hear him whistling through his teeth in that way he had.

Baby was getting well fast, and one morning I decided to make a pan of chocolate fudge and take her and it down to the shed. When I started walking down the dirt road to the barns, I heard

Callie and Raider let out a big whoop, and I could tell that it was all that they could do to keep from throwing down the handful of tobacco they held. They were almost done with the truck, though, and there wasn't another one in sight, so they hurriedly finished it. I held out the fudge dish, and Raider was the first one to get to it. He grabbed a piece and started rolling his eyes. He ran his tongue around the edge of it, getting the grains of sugar in the corners of his mouth. The plate emptied quickly, and Callie, wanting to prolong the party, said, "Let's get a watermelon, too." She ran out to the edge of the field and got one from the shadiest spot she could find. It was still hot, though, when we busted it and Callie picked up a piece with her black, tobacco-gummy fingers.

"I thought hot watermelon'd kill you," Raider said.

Old Mama spoke up. "That ain't hot watermelon there, that there's *warm* watermelon."

Raider said, "Oh," and bit in. We all broke out laughing. All the tension that had built up had made us silly. When Callie made a face as the bitter tobacco gum on her hands got in the watermelon, I told her to quit eating so fast and stop and wash her hands off with some tomatoes that would cut the gum. I could tell that Old Mama was about to launch into some story about somebody dying from eating hot watermelon when we heard the rumble of the tobacco truck, loud and close to us. I glanced up quickly to see which one it was and looked right into Jack's eyes.

* * *

I was sitting, rocking in the kitchen, the wood of the chair pressing against my legs as I sat shelling butter beans from the big aluminum pan that we had bought down at Haw Landing when we first got married. Aaron was stretched out on the daybed that we kept in the kitchen during putting-in time, reading the day's paper. I remembered standing at the front door, watching the mailman put the paper in the box in front of the yard, and not bothering to go take it out, thinking whatever there is in the paper, what has it got to do with me, my life?

Jack had gone on down to the barn to take care of the fires as soon as he'd finished his supper, and Baby was, I thanked the Lord, asleep in her crib in the bedroom.

As I shelled, I glanced over at Aaron. His bare white feet looked so vulnerable; the bones, the little ones going to his toes, were like an ivory fan I'd seen in Ruth's trunk. He arched and moved one foot and then set in motion the nervous twitch I'd noticed that his daddy had, the thump of the big toe against the toe beside it, a motion probably unnoticed by the person doing it but as irritating to the person watching as the steady drip of a faucet. It didn't irritate me right then, though. Since the night before I'd been feeling tender toward him. The night before was as strange as anything that had happened in the last few strange months. Suddenly after weeks of strain, we had become close in the dark, his hands and mouth had searched with a motion and rhythm like silk from evening spiders. We both seemed to be searching over and over, communicating things that words could never say. I saw him again as the clean good boy I had first seen standing at the edge of the cemetery at Cobb Swamp Church.

I looked at his hands and feet for a long time and thought of the time after Baby was born when the doctor had cautioned us to wait six weeks, and in the fifth week, without speaking of it, we had come together and for a while nothing else mattered. How had I come so far from that? How had I let these things happen to me with Jack? Aaron and I had struck a bargain together, and I'd meant to keep it. Had I turned bad because I was lonesome and liked to hear words whispered to me, words like "pretty," words like "smart"?

I kept sitting there looking at Aaron for a long time. I wondered that he didn't feel my eyes on him, didn't know my thoughts. But then I didn't know his, did I? I wanted to, had tried, asked, begged, but there was such a big part of himself that he wouldn't or couldn't share. Maybe all men are like that. I thought of Daddy. Thought of Jack. I looked at Aaron's face, the dark lashes around his eyes. How could I have ever done those things to him? If he could even imagine Jack and me lying in each other's arms the hot nights at the barn when he and Baby lay asleep, and me trying to slip in and wash myself so that he wouldn't notice the cured-tobacco smell thick on my skin, what would he do? If he could imagine . . . Could regular people like Aaron imagine such things? I have to stop all this, straighten things out and try again. If me and Baby got lonesome we were just going to have to stand it.

"Roxy—" The word shattered the sound of the ticking clock. Aaron was speaking to me and had startled me out of my thoughts. "There's something Daddy wants me to talk to you about."

He had turned and was sitting on the side of the couch, picking up his shoes and socks. The expression on his face was odd, and he wasn't looking directly at me. My heart jumped, and I felt dizzy and reached for the butter-bean pan for balance. Some of the shells scattered across the floor. I looked at them lying at my feet. They were the best butter beans to come out of the garden all summer. Things might have been bad for us at the house, but the crops took no notice of it. They just kept right on growing.

I waited for him to go on talking—knowing that he couldn't be rushed or prompted, that he would say whatever he had to say in his own good time—but I felt my uneasiness looming up in the room like another person.

"Daddy mentioned something about Jack staying here." Aaron talked fast now, pushing the words out in a rush. "It might be better . . . he said that we ought to get the first tobacco to market and then give him some money and send him on . . ."

I was afraid to say anything, afraid my voice

would give out on me. I just kept sitting there, looking down at the hulls on the floor, nodding.

"I've already told him, Roxy, told Jack that after the opening sale we'll be able to manage without him . . . I hated to do it, why don't you tell him too?"

He paused, sat there with his head down staring at his feet, as if he was waiting for me to speak, protest or something, but I couldn't bring myself to say a word. In a way this was what I wanted, for him to make a move to stop the things that were going on and, on the other hand, the thought of Jack's really leaving . . . I couldn't imagine . . . how could I just let him leave . . . ?

"Somebody at the church mentioned to the folks that it didn't look right with you and Jack in the same house all the time . . . that you might start noticing each other . . ." His voice sounded low and embarrassed as he said the last words. In a minute he looked up at me, his eyes solemn, but making an effort to make his voice lighter, he said, "Talk to Jack about it. I hated to tell him. He told me he was counting on staying through the winter. Tell him how it looks for you, Roxy. It might be better."

I sat for a long time after Aaron left the room. I heard him fall into a hard sleep, the sounds coming into the kitchen where I sat rocking and tapping my leg with the fly swatter, trying to think what to do, what to say. I knew I had to go to the barn. I got up, and once I smoothed my skirt and started walking down the dirt path I moved quickly with a purpose. As I walked, I could see little sparks in the smoke going up into the night like drunk lightning bugs, and as I got near the barn the heavy, sweet smell of the curing tobacco hit my nostrils. I could almost taste it—the syrupy, musty smell like bodies making love in the heat. A drug in itself, just the smell of it.

There wasn't a light at the barn. The glint of the lanterns showed once in a while like pictures of a ship, but they weren't lit. The only light was from the fires at the two barns. They crackled and moved and hypnotized me. I don't know anything as spellbinding as a fire except maybe clouds on a day when the wind moves them along so fast that they change shapes constantly and the eye can't leave for fascination.

When I came close enough to feel the heat from the fire, the mosquitoes stopped gnawing at my legs and arms. My eyes made out Jack's form lying on the cot, sprawled out, face down. He didn't speak, but I knew he watching me and playing possum. He let me get almost up to him, and then with a laugh he lunged up, grabbed me around the waist, boosted me into the air and shook me like a rag doll. We fell laughing into each other. I was laughing in spite of myself, laughing into his chest, forgetting for the moment why I had come to the barn.

I said, "You smell like a tow sack, you smell just like that old tow sack you've been lying on."

He didn't answer, just kept pulling my face into his chest, mashing my words flat against him.

"Jack, Jack . . ."

"Ummm" . . . mocking, teasing.

Pulling me down in spite of my efforts to talk, to protest that I came to talk, to tell him something important; pulling me onto the tobacco-truck bed, covering me with mosquito net, bending over me, holding my face still, putting his fingers on my lips every time I tried to talk. Bending over my face, smoothing the skin of it with tobacco-stained fingers, making me taste the tobacco, making round motions on my cheekbones, tracing the light from the fire on them. Saying, no laughing in his voice, "You, you're the tobacco princess. You're prettier than any Ava."

I couldn't think straight, couldn't help but see how the firelight made the gold colors of his skin glow, couldn't help but think he was from some other world or time and that nothing else was real except the two of us on the rough bed, lava from an ancient volcano.

I heard him whisper in my ear, "Don't worry, he's not coming down here."

Later we lay still, and I told him what I had gone down there to tell him. We lay there looking at each other. Something unspeakable and strange went between us.

And then early, very early, before the sun was up, I left him, got up and ran up the road, the heavy dew soaking my bare legs and cotton broomstick skirt, ran lightly so as not to disturb the chickens, slipped as quietly as a cowboy from an old-time picture show into the house. I washed myself, combed and wound up my hair and stood in the kitchen in fresh starched clothes, cooking eggs in fried-meat grease when the house woke up. I kept my face expressionless the way I had learned to keep it early in the summer—back inside myself, not reaching out to make things right for Aaron, jealously guarding the secrets inside me from outsiders.

Aaron got up and made his usual morning noises as he washed in the basin in the kitchen, sounds that this morning grated at my nerves. His slow ritual seemed to me to go on and on. I was impatient to see him out the door so I could have moments to myself to lie across the bed and think and collect the night before in my mind and rest a few minutes.

"Did you talk to Jack?" he asked in a matter-of-fact voice.

I had anticipated the words, and I tried to sound as matter-of-fact as he did. "Yes," not "Yes, and he's not going to do it," or "Yes, and Lord knows what's going to happen now," or "Yes, and now the fat's really in the fire," but just "Yes." And he accepted that and went into the day, and it seemed that it was all taken care of as simply as hitching the mule to the tobacco truck and heading on out to the field.

And that's the way it stayed. The days were the same in shape as they had been before Baby was burned and before Aaron had spoken—wake up, work, eat, sleep, and sometimes nights in the firelight at the barns.

No more was said about leaving. I reckoned, if I reckoned anything, that Aaron was expecting Jack to be gone after opening day. I would hear Aaron whistling when he shaved, the whistle with no melody that I used to think was contentment but that I was beginning to see meant nothing at all except that his lips moved and the thin sound came out.

I didn't know what Jack aimed to do. For all I knew he would be gone. I walked through those days with a tight rock of fear in my stomach. The feeling made me think of the time in the dark upstairs at Daddy's house right after Georgeanna had died when I went to stay there and slept with Callie in her room. The time when the big, hulking third husband of Gyp got mad. Gyp, who always seemed strong as a lion, told Ruth about how scared she was of him, how he was crazy when he was drunk, said she didn't know what he was going to do to her. Overhearing the conversation from the top of the stairs, I envisioned sharp ice picks and bloody-boned things. And Gyp had asked to sleep at the house until she could get something settled between them. She had stayed there in the little room at the end of the hall upstairs where we were, and in the nights every sound, every twig, every strike from the courthouse clock brought live lightning to me as I sat on the long bed in the long room

staring at the long windows that went all the way
down to the floor and overlooked the street. A
pigeon-rustle in the eaves was all it took. Long
after Gyp and the man had gotten their "divorce"
and he'd left town on the back of a coal truck headed
to Detroit (according to Gyp), every time I walked
up those stairs I carried the feeling of axes in the
night with me. It was then that I told Aaron
Walston that yes, I would like to marry him and
make a home, a safe home where I could lie in the
shelter of his arms.

What happened was the last thing I expected.
Aaron started talking about taking me and Baby on
a little trip. He started talking about it when they
came back from town on the opening day of the
market.

Jack and Aaron had taken the tobacco out of the
packhouse where we had all graded it and tied it
the day before. They wrapped it in big bundles with
sheets made of sewed-together tow sacks. Handing
it back and forth to each other, they piled part of the
cured crop on one truck and another big pile on the
flatbed truck.

When they came in from the market that night,
they looked pleased and happy and about half
drunk. We all sat around the kitchen table and ate
the hot dogs they brought back from the Greek's.
Aaron talked on and on about the price his tobacco
had brought in. Jack sat and smiled down at the

cards he kept shuffling and spreading across the table.

Aaron kept on talking, and Jack kept on shuffling, and when I sat back down after I'd cleared the paper off the table, the words and the sound of the cards took on a rhythm and I drifted off thinking about the tobacco auction. I'd always wanted to go to one. I had the same feeling about an auction as I did about a blacksmith's shop and about the train station where Georgeanna used to take me to watch the big black train come in. I was drawn by the huddle of men that I imagined were in the warehouses during the auction, talking secret talk that only men could understand. There wasn't a chance of me going because they always said, "Warehouse's no place for a woman." But I could see it in my mind, the men reared back smoking cigars and talking about their tobacco, speculating about the price it would bring that day, talking about what a hard-working year it had been, the hardest ever. They'd be walking up and down the aisles stroking the leaves lightly, breathing in the smell of it. Quiet men that hardly ever talked about anything, let alone brag, bragging about how fine their crops are. I could just hear Mr. Wainwright, or the warehouseman at whatever the warehouse, throwing out a bid just to get things going. "Bid 'er up," he'd say and then name a price.

After he'd say a price, the auctioneer would pick that up and chant it over and over until somebody else would pick up the bidding, and then he'd chant that. While he'd chant, he'd keep walking and everybody'd follow him, the men from all the tobacco companies that had come there to bid on the best bright-leaf tobacco in the world. His eyes would dart around, and he'd manage to keep them on each person and know what he was bidding. All without missing a beat in his song. The buyers from the different companies had funny little ways to signal when they wanted to bid. "Do I hear a five, a five, a five?" might be answered by a raised finger, a nod of the head or even a wink. I had heard Daddy say that one time there was a fellow from the American Tobacco Company who could wiggle his ears when the price was right for him.

The clock's ticking in our kitchen seemed like part of the rhythm. As we sat at the table, Aaron sort of pinched me, and I jumped when I realized that he was talking to me. "It's Wainwright's they're using for the dance tomorrow night, Roxy."

It really surprised me that he mentioned the dance. I had been trying ever since we'd been married to talk to him about the Tobacco Festival. I'd never really been to one. Georgeanna used to take me downtown to watch, but we always stayed at the edge of the crowd. I'd tried to mention it to Aaron, but it seemed like he was always just staring into the tobacco fields. Besides going out every single morning before he'd even eaten breakfast and walking up and down the rows bending down to examine a plant, a leaf, he just seemed to want to talk about it all the time. Once or twice when I'd see him out like that, I'd ask him what he was doing, and he's say soft and dreamy, "Just studying it, just studying it. I love to see it grow." And then after barning time, I'd see him take a leaf fresh-cured from the barn and hold it in his hand up to his face and slowly breathe the smell of it in with his eyes closed. Then he'd hold it out, smooth it, stroke it slowly and tell me to touch it, saying, "Ain't that nice, Roxy? Ain't that nice? Feels just like a kid glove."

Looking over at me now, he saw my surprise. "I don't see any reason we can't go. Get Baby ready early. We can get up early and go on in and take in all the festival. Then next week, after I get some business straight, I don't see why we can't go to Carolina Beach for a day or two."

I sucked in my breath. He paused and rolled a cigarette and added, "Jack can look after things here."

There was a dead silence. Not a sound. Not even a snore from Baby, who was fast asleep in her Kiddie Koop with her round behind sticking up in the air like a bug. I sat there waiting, and I felt a kind of silver tension as the three of us sat there. I hesitated to look up at either one of them. After a while, Jack stood up and made a sort of shaking noise with his clothes and walked outside. When I glanced over at Aaron, he had a real strange expression on his face, the same sort of look in a way that he'd had when he said his tobacco had brought top dollar. It wasn't until late that night after we had already gone to bed that I heard Jack come inside and go into his room.

We got up bright and early just like Aaron said we should. Baby was excited when she saw me putting her sun-suits in a suitcase and heard us talking about the parade. Callie and Raider had been telling her about the pageant all summer, and she knew that she was in for something really different from the routine days on the farm. After breakfast was over and we had the things in the car, I went over to the packhouse to see if I could see anything of Jack. He hadn't come in to eat, and I didn't want to leave without at least seeing him. Aaron had gone down to the barn to check on something. I didn't see Jack at first, but when I walked into the dim packhouse, I heard a noise in the back, a scratching like a rat. When I got closer, I saw Jack bending over, poking at a wasp's nest that was in the corner. I blurted out, "You're going to get stung!" as if I were talking to Baby. He whirled around, and when I saw his face I stepped back. His face was streaked with mud, the same the wasps had used to build their nests. His lips traced in clay were white.

"God *damn* it, Roxy." He jerked out his arm and grabbed the back of my neck and kissed me hard, cutting my lip with his teeth from the force. I started crying and leaned up against the side of the packhouse to get my balance and to brush the mud and blood from my face before Aaron came back.

Jack left the low building with a lunge.

* * *

When Aaron got there, I was sitting in the car with Baby. I kept a handkerchief against my lips for a while, and he didn't notice the little nick in my lip. I was so stirred by Jack's actions that I wasn't able to notice anything until we got into town. By the time I pulled my thoughts in, we were riding down Cash Street, where Baby was pointing at bush after bush of crepe myrtle, waving at the puffy pink blooms, saying, "Wa' melon." I hugged her to me.

The smell of the town, heavy with the sweetness of thousands of pounds of cured tobacco, hit me, and I leaned my head on the side of the window and shut my eyes and drank in the richness. That smell at harvest time every year gave me a feeling that nothing else did—a feeling so strong that I wanted to reach out and hug the whole world tight.

We passed by the funeral home, but there wasn't a soul on the porch. I guessed that everybody was busy getting ready for the parade one way or the other. Even Strother was probably brushing his old army uniform.

When we turned the corner into Robert E. Lee Street and first caught sight of the house, I realized that with all the strange things that had happened this summer, my view of things had changed a lot. The house looked different to me. I guess I had always resented it so much that I hadn't really seen it. The porch was wide and the banisters were white and graceful and closed in the porch like fencing in a little garden. Big green rocking chairs sat rocking by themselves in the little breeze that stirred from the pecan trees in the front yard. The wide carport stretched out and had white lattice-work around it like a ribbon. Off the porch from the other side I could see the glass door and window that was the sunporch where Daddy stayed when he was at the house. I smiled when I thought of the pile of detective magazines and Chesterfield ciga-rettes that I knew were stacked in there. As we got out of the car and walked up the steps, we could see our reflections in the wavy glass of the long, low window that reached to the floor of the porch. I put my finger to the doorbell to make the sound that would ring under the big round table in the dining room for Gyp to answer. We were greeted only with pigeons and mourning doves' sad sounds and rus-tles from the side door. Soon, though, Callie came busting through the door with Raider right behind her.

Callie nearly knocked me down, saying, "Look here at my dress, Roxy." It was red-and-white seersucker, and she had been talking about it all summer. I turned Baby's finger loose and felt the material.

"It's pretty. When did you get it?"

"I went by yesterday after we got home and paid the last dollar." She smiled. She had told me how much she wanted to buy something with her own tobacco money.

"Why don't we go to the Mother and Daughter store and buy you a new one for the parade?" I glanced down at the perfectly good cotton with little flowers that Estelle had made for me and hesitated. "Come on, Roxy! Let's get you something red." I glanced over at Aaron, who had picked up the *News and Observer* and sat down in a rocking chair.

"Do you have time to take us, Aaron?"

He nodded yes and reached in his pocket and pulled out a ten-dollar bill and indicated that I should take it. It shook me a little because Aaron was funny about money, and even when he was pushed to admit that Baby and I needed some personal thing he would react by throwing the money down on a dresser or bed, and it never was quite enough to take care of everything. I didn't understand that part of him at all. I didn't have any idea what he did with the money he made every year on the crop. But today he seemed eager to please. "Get a bright-red one, Roxy; it'll set off your hair."

"Where's Ruth?" I asked.

Callie said she was at Pender's getting a few more groceries and would be back in a little while. I went back to the kitchen and spoke to Gyp and gave her the tomatoes and other things that we'd brought from the garden.

Gyp said, "You ain't picked up a bit. In fact I believe you've fell off."

I just shook my head and said, "It's been too hot to eat, Gyp."

I went out and sat down in the swing to wait for Ruth to come back. The parade was to start at three, so we had plenty of time to go buy a dress, eat a little bit of dinner and be down there to get a good place to stand. Raider, who was sitting on the edge of the flower boxes that Ruth had full of pink petunias, said, "Who busted you in the mouth, Roxy?" I glanced up quickly at Aaron to see if he'd heard, but he was studying the newspaper and didn't pay any attention.

I said, "Oh, I bumped against the packhouse door . . . I'm hot, let's go get a Co-Cola."

After I moved around a little and got over my embarrassed feeling, my eyes fell on Aaron, still reading. He looked so good sitting there shaved with his hair clean and shiny and curling around his ears. It made me think of when I first knew him and he talked with a sureness that made my heart sing. Where had that sureness gone? He walked around the farm staring at the field, dressed like a tenant all the time, and never let me see the boy that I had liked to begin with. It seemed to me that at times he acted more like an old woman than anything else. I'd thought at the time we got married that men got out and did things, made things happen, but life on the farm was just one long hard day after another.

He must have felt my eyes on him because he put the paper down and smiled at me and beckoned me over and pulled me down to whisper to me. "I'll drop y'all off at the store. You get that red seersucker dress and get a bathing suit too. I can't see any reason we can't ride on down to Carolina Beach."

91

I flushed. I didn't know how to take this new mood. When we left for the parade, I had on the new puckered dress that fit me real well, and Callie had helped me pull my hair back to one side like a picture we saw in one of Ruth's magazines. It was not until we were sitting on the funeral-home porch ready for the parade that I ran my tongue over the cut on my lip and thought of Jack again. I wondered what he was doing, what he was thinking. Strother kept trying to get his rocker as close to mine as possible and reaching over and patting me on the leg and saying how he hadn't seen me in a long time. He felt the material over my thigh and said, "I love your outfit."

Neb came out on the porch and walked up and down like a nervous cat. I liked to look at Neb. He always walked like he was hearing some real good music in his head that nobody else was hearing. He kept glancing over at me, and I knew he was wanting to ask me where Jack was, but he never did, and I never said. For all I knew, Jack might be coming in for the pageant. I quickly pushed that thought out of my head.

Out at the stadium where Daddy and the boys always go to ball games, all the lights were on full blast. After a year of planning and waiting, the Tobacco Pageant had begun. Half the town had costumes and was marching and dancing and strutting around. The Chesterfield float brought the Hollywood Big Band leader and his band out into the middle of the field. And for the grand finale, all the tobacco princesses paraded out, one by one. The one that had been chosen for the queen was brought out last to be crowned. The float she rode on was like a dream, and she was beautiful. The lights shone on her arms and made them as smooth as moonlight. Her dress hung around her in gold folds. It was like a hoop skirt from the Civil War days, layers and layers of big skirt over hoops, and the layers were all made out of golden tobacco leaves, leaves cured the brightest color. They lay like petals on a rose. Her long, dark hair hung down over her shoulders. *Ava*, I heard her name whispered and echoed through the crowd. As the crown was placed on her head, everybody in the stadium slowly stood up like people in the seventh-inning stretch at a ball game. And everybody started singing "The Star-Spangled Banner" while fireworks were shot off. It made goose bumps go up and down my arms. I drew close to Aaron, putting my arm against him as the sky rockets flared up. I was almost in a trance while we walked out with the crowd pushing us along. I jumped when Callie and Raider ran up from the field in their costumes.

Only once or twice had I thought that I'd seen a bright head in the corners.

There hadn't been any sign of Jack when we came in Sunday night, and I felt a flurry when I realized how little I'd thought about him since we'd been gone.

I was out on the back doorstep early Monday morning, throwing corn to the chickens, when he came into the yard. I guess he'd slept at the barn even though there wasn't any tobacco curing.

He called out to me, and I was surprised at the light sound of his voice. Loving and teasing—the last way I'd expected him to be. Asking about the festival and everything. He acted sweet and friendly to Aaron when he came out, too. His voice sounded like June. All of us standing out there laughing and talking in the sun, as if the summer had turned around and gone back and was starting all over again.

Aaron said, "Jack, ride with me over to Daddy's. I've got to go over some figures with him this morning before we go to the beach. You can drive the truck I'm buying from him back over here."

Before they left, Jack called over his shoulder to me, "Roxy, since we missed Sunday dinner yesterday, how about frying two chickens tonight and making some creamed potatoes?" For some reason I felt pleased so I nodded at him and turned to Aaron and said, "You hear him, Aaron, so be sure you get back in time for supper."

After Jack dropped Aaron off, I heard the sound of the new truck as he passed the house and went down to the barn area. He stayed down there all day and that gave me a chance to catch up on the washing and get the house cleaned before I had to start on the supper. I kept humming all day, remembering the music and lights and everything in town. I thought, "Maybe the bad is over. Maybe we can forget, just forget everything that's happened this summer and start all over. Maybe we can somehow just eat and laugh, and they can play their music together again."

But that night after we had eaten all the chicken and were still sitting around the table gnawing on the crusty chicken feet that I had fried up, Jack turned to Aaron and said with a kind of a high, light voice, "Come on with me down back of the barn, Aaron. I want you to see something I killed down there today. I don't know what it is, but it's something strange. A strange animal."

And right then as I sat there in the dim light, I had one of those little spells that I have. As if a bird with wide wings flew right close to my head and flapped his wings, and nobody could hear it but me.

When Jack reached over to the shelf and picked up his rifle and they walked out the door into the night, any words I had to say stayed inside me with the flapping of wings. I never even thought then that there hadn't been any shot fired on the place that day.

When the screen door slammed, my back was to it. I had Baby sitting up on the washstand stripped off, and I was giving her a good lathering before I sat her down in the tub on the floor to rinse her off. The way she toddled and crawled around all day sliding on that one leg like she did in that crazy way, no

matter how often I scrubbed her I never could seem
to get her quite clean. It was so good to see her
scooting around across the floor like that again after
seeing her slowed and pulled by the puckered burns
that I couldn't make myself fuss with her about
much. The way she was wiggling and squirming—
she didn't want to be held back, she wanted to go
when she was ready—made me think of Georgeanna sitting with her hat on early in the morning
waiting for the stores to open so she could go as
soon as anybody cracked open a door or cranked up
a car.

I was trying to hold Baby still long enough to look
at the scars to see how they were healing when I
heard the door slam behind me.

"Aaron, Aaron, look . . ." I began.

"Aaron's not here."

It was Jack's voice. I turned around then and
realized that he was alone.

He kept standing there, with his long arms
hanging straight down by his side, looking at me in
a strange, intent way. I had never seen him look
like that before.

"Get Baby's clothes on, we've got to go," he said.

"Go where?"

He suddenly started shaking and trembling like I
had never seen anybody do before.

"Don't ask me what, *don't ask me what*, get your
clothes and put some things in a suitcase. We got to
go. *Now*."

He walked over to me and put his hands slowly

up to my shoulders. I didn't know what he was going to do, but he gave me a little shake and sort of pushed me toward the bedroom.

"Take that!" He pointed to the little suitcase that was sitting on the floor, the one that I'd packed to carry to Carolina Beach.

His voice was ragged, and a bolt of fear shot through me. Baby knew something was strange too and came over and clung to my legs and begged to be taken.

"Where's Aaron?"

He just looked at me, hard and funny.

He went up to the front of the house and I could hear him in the spare room getting some things together. In a matter of minutes he was back in the kitchen, and as he went out the screen door to the car he said, "Get ready, Roxy."

I saw that he really meant it. He came back in an grabbed my elbow and said, "Get in that car." We left everything just the way it had been when he came in: the bathwater and washrag there on the washstand; the windows open; everything. We had a few clothes and diapers for Baby, and that was about all. He did reach up and pull the string to cut the light off. But when we got to the steps I held tight to Baby and stopped with my heels hard.

"I want to know where Aaron is, Jack. This isn't funny."

He looked sharp at me and said, "You don't really want to know, Roxy, but if you do, he went over to his daddy's in the new truck. I'll tell you about it later. Now, get in."

I knew something was wrong. Bad wrong. One minute I was standing there soaping Baby and the next I was being pushed into the car. I couldn't seem to get my thoughts straight; they kept jumping around like little musical notes on a white page. But all my instincts told me that it wasn't going to do any good to keep questioning Jack now. He was wild-eyed, and I thought I better go along with what he wanted to do, for a while anyway. As we drove out of the yard it came to the front of my mind that not only had Aaron not come back with Jack, but the rifle hadn't come back either.

We drove all night. The Studebaker that Aaron had bought when we got married was still a good car, and we didn't meet many people on the night road. Jack drove like a hurled knife, swift and sure. We only stopped once, right before dawn, when I kept after him about Baby's diaper. There was a little service station in South Carolina that was just opening up. South Carolina—that name seemed so strange to me; it was hard to believe that there could be another Carolina. I could hear the men, my daddy, Aaron's daddy, that had lived in our area all their lives, saying "C'lina." It didn't seem real to me that there could be a south part to it.

I took Baby to the toilet, and when we came out Jack was walking around by the gas pump. He got us all an orange drink but said to hurry. I never had been out of the state of North Carolina before, and as it started to get light I noticed different kinds of trees and plants growing along the side of the road. I was still very upset about where we were going and what we were going to do because Jack hadn't told me any more about what was going on, just kept saying, "Trust me." Part of me wondered why Aaron had let him take the car, but there was a little feeling of thrill, adventure in that part. Another part of me, like a wet gray stone right in the middle of my chest, knew that some dreadful thing had happened and that any minute I would have the truth thrown in my face like a spotlight. But I was used to a feeling of dread, I had been born with it, so when the most dreadful things happened, the feeling of dread had been there so long that the shock was dulled some for me. It was that way when Georgeanna died. Her actual death wasn't as painful for me as the times when I lay awake at night imagining it. Even Baby being scalded, when it actually happened, wasn't as horrible as all the times that I'd feared she'd be hurt—fall on the sharp plow, have her eyes pecked out by a rooster. The accident wasn't as bad at the time as my everyday imaginings, and then the part after—the looking at and accepting the tender pink flesh in the night in my mind.

We drove on into Georgia. Jack started pointing out things, sort of slow and kind, his eyes squinting in the early morning light. We were alone in the front seat now. Baby was sleeping in the back seat, tired from peeping out the window in the dark to see only an occasional car light, satisfied for the time being by the orange drink and the clean diaper. I sat with my hands in my lap, and once in a while he'd reach over for my hand and rub it with a little sad rub and point out something he knew I'd never seen before.

I was nodding when he said, "If I remember right, there's a place up here off the road where there's a spring we can drink out of." He spotted a place where he thought it was, and we pulled off and stopped and got out of the car and left Baby asleep. We stretched ourselves, and after we drank the clear cold water that spurted out and washed our faces with it, we looked around at the cool green place. It was what I thought an oasis would be like. Wild ferns grew all around the water, and I could see violets, though they weren't blooming, and the small kind of morning-glory vines that take off and grow all over everything. It was getting really light now, and the tender rays shone through the leaves. Everything was still. We could have been hundreds of years back in time if it hadn't been for the car sitting there. Jack was standing behind me, and he reached for me, his arms coming around me, light like the wild plants, touching my waist, tracing across my hipbones, my stomach, then up to my breasts as soft and tender and wild as the taste of green grass in your mouth. He said, "Shh . . . look!" It was a big white bird rising from the deep woods behind us. We could hear the flap of his wings.

"It's a crane."

"How do you know?"

"We're in Georgia now. Not too far from where I was raised."

I was hard to imagine anything bad in the world as we stood there holding each other, and I didn't let myself think.

We didn't drive too far after that before we came to a place where Jack slowed and turned in. There was a wooden sign that said "Cypress Tree Travelers' Camp," and when I glanced over to Jack to ask him what we were doing, he pointed out some beautiful strange-looking trees sitting in the watery place and told me they were cypresses. All the ground around the camp looked sandy, and I saw a woman in a flowered cotton dress and apron out there sweeping the yard with a big yard broom. Dominecker chickens scurried under her feet, and a few minutes after we drove up and stopped the only sound to be heard was the engine sighing and the chickens puck-pucking our arrival.

Jack got out and walked over to her and said something, then came on back and drove me and Baby over to the cabin farthest away from the road.

We went in and didn't do much looking around or anything else, just put our things inside and fell into the bed.

When we woke up, the afternoon sun was streaking in the window, and Baby was standing there looking out at the chickens and fussing back at them because her diaper was sopping and a little line of ants had come in the door and was crawling on her bare toes.

Jack got up grouchy and said, "Stay here." He left and came back after a while with a plate of dinner, smoked sausage and peas and cornbread. We ate, and he said, "Stay here," and looked at me real hard. After he went out the door of the cabin, I heard the car crank up. He was gone a long time. Baby and I stayed in the cabin and didn't know quite what to do so we just played the radio that was in there.

He came back about midnight, and I tried to start asking questions. I was standing in my underskirt when he came in; my dress smelled sour and I had hung it up to air out. I hadn't thought to get any other clothes for myself when we left, just the bunch of things for Baby. Jack had some things rolled up, but I didn't bother them because he was real funny about anybody touching his things. I'd made a big pallet for Baby, and she was stretched out on it, asleep.

"Jack, you've got to tell me something."

He looked different somehow. Sad around the eyes. He reached out his arms to me.

"I need to go home, Jack."

But it was as if he wasn't hearing any words at all. He looked at me with a strange kind of light in his eyes, like somebody with a fever. He slowly slid his hands down my arms and bent his head until his mouth touched the little hollow place between my shoulder blades and my breast, my weakest spot, the place where I have the most feeling. He was slow and deliberate and different than I'd ever known him to be, grave and powerful, and when I tried weakly to protest he closed his wide hand around the back of my neck and forced me down on the bed. It was like two other people. Above the sounds we were making, I could hear the freight train whistle way off.

But when it was over and he sat in the chair by the side of the bed, the tears ran down my face and I said, "Jack, I need to go home."

He said, "After you see what's on my overalls you won't want to go back," and I knew what he meant without him saying it.

I knew what he meant when he said, "I can't keep it any longer."

My mind had not consciously known until this minute, but I knew now. "You hurt Aaron." As I tried to speak, my throat closed up.

"I hit him not too far from the hole."

The room seemed to vibrate and tilt. Again I tried to speak, the words sticking in my throat. "Wha, what hole . . . what?"

"I hit him, Aaron, twice . . . at the hole . . . I dug the hole."

Then he started talking really fast, getting up and moving around the room, walking in circles. Saying how he had dug a big hole, a grave, while we were in town Saturday, how he had dug it and then sat and looked into it all day and night while we were gone.

"I called him out there and hit him with the rifle and threw him in the hole and covered him up."

I got up and stood against the wall as far on the other side of the room as I could. In my mind I saw in a flash of light their two faces in the dark near the barns. Aaron's long and narrow, the cheekbones hard and sharp, sharp like my hipbones, the dark, heavy brows growing almost together, protecting the eyes that had all the colors of green and brown in them, saw them look at Jack as they always did, straight, straight like looking far off, but then change and look the look of surprise as he saw Jack raise the gun.

And Jack—the face that always seemed so carved, so sure; I saw the twist of the lip and then the bottom lip pull tight across his teeth as he lifted his arm and let out a sharp sound.

My mind whirled. It was as if I felt the blows myself. Knocking, stunning, unbalancing. Sounds came out of my mouth as I fell onto the bed.

Then for a long space we didn't talk. We just lay across the bed, and neither of us said anything. About dawn he reached out and put an arm across me. It felt heavy like Papa's overcoat that George-anna used to lay across me when I was little and fell asleep on the couch.

I woke up when the sun came up. It took me a few minutes to figure out where I was.

I can't say how I felt, hollow I guess. When I turned over and looked at his face, I realized that his face was back on his face and mine was back on mine. I traced my fingers over my own face to be certain, and sure enough I felt my features there, my own high cheekbones and no birthmark. I wasn't him anymore. I remembered hearing Georgeanna describe the time when she had scarlet fever. She said, "I lay a year, a whole year, on the bed, and it was like I was away in another land. Was this the Land of Canaan? And one day it was like I woke up and looked out the window where the pane had just been washed, and I recognized everything again."

I kept looking at the face that was now strange to me. What thoughts were inside that head? Why had this happened? How could it have happened? I'd always thought I had a lot of understanding, that I could put myself into anybody's shoes. I thought that I'd gotten this trait from Daddy. How lucky, I used to think, the people were who came to him at the funeral home, all confused and grieving, to have that understanding man there to help them. But I wondered about this ability now as I looked at Jack, because I didn't understand. I didn't understand at all. Yes, the things that Jack and I did were terrible and wrong, the way we had behaved all summer, but it was alive. This was dead. Whatever I'd had in mind during those months, wasting life wasn't it. Lord knows I knew how it felt to be crazy from jealousy, to feel left out, but I could no more have planned to kill somebody than I could have deliberately gone off and left Baby alone in this cabin in Georgia.

I was still lying there thinking, "What am I doing in this tourist camp in Georgia with this strange person?" when he stirred. I tried to move out from under his arm to get the weight off me. He woke up and looked straight at me, and for a minute I was terrified.

This man had murdered Aaron Earl Walston, beat him, beat him over the head. But he was only reaching for his cigarettes.

"We'd better be leaving here." His voice sounded deep and tired.

I knew that he meant that we had better keep moving in case somebody had found Aaron's body and had started after us.

For the first time since we had left home, I thought about Daddy. I imagined his anguish when somebody told him about Aaron and that I was gone. What had I been thinking of to come off like this? How had I let this thing happen between Jack and Aaron? How had Daddy let it happen? How had Aaron let it happen? But most of all, how had *I* let it happen? Me. Me. How had I let it happen? How could I have been so weak and drifting to let it come to this? Me and Baby off down in Georgia somewhere with a strange man that had come into our life off the back of a freight train and hurt Aaron and got us way down here.

Time hung, and I didn't know how long I lay

looking at him before I realized, how long before the thought got into my brain that not only was I lying in bed in a tourist camp with a lean man with sleep cracklings in his eyes and spit in the edge of his mouth and moisture on the pillow where he'd slept, but he expected me, was expecting me to leave with him this morning to *stay* . . . to run from the sheriff, my daddy, everything I knew.

As I was recoiling from the thought as if it were a snake, he spoke low with what now seemed to me to sound like a little whine in his voice. "Roxy, I'll treat you right."

A feeling began to bubble up in me slowly.

"Say you'll be ready to go, Roxy; say it."

I couldn't speak. I felt dumb, shy, self-conscious. The way I'd always felt when I tried to look directly at somebody and say anything, let alone "no." I had never thought of it before, but I had never said no to anybody about anything in my life, except to Aaron on the Fourth of July, and look what happened then. I had just avoided the subject or left the room or done anything to keep peace. And as I realized this, I also realized that nearly everybody I lived around had always acted the same way. Aaron had. He acted the same way I did, rebelling by making love with me, but he never did stand up to his mother and say, "No, I'm not going off to the college because that's not what I want to do with my life," and when it came time to tell Jack to leave the farm, he didn't run Jack off by saying, "Jack, I want you to leave my farm, my wife, because things have gotten out of hand." Instead he had said to me, "I think it would be better . . . you make him go. I hate to." He could have faced Jack and sent him on his way even if he lost me, lost Jack in doing it. But the worst, somehow the very worst thought of all, was that I realized that Daddy probably was just as bad about facing an unpleasant thing. I could see him, one hand in a baggy pants pocket, his watch swinging, see him slap his crumpled hat on his head, push at the screen door going to the escape of the funeral home, mumbling, "To hell, to hell with the whole damn thing."

He did it too, left the room when Ruth was talking, to keep from having to say no, turned his back on things like he had done on the farm this summer. Anything to keep peace. Until this minute I had thought that Daddy was like God, but I knew now that he was just a man and at times he was as weak as everybody else, and I realized he wasn't going to work some miracle that would make everything right, make Aaron well, get me and Baby out of this mess here in the tourist camp. I was going to have to do it myself. I was here alone, and I had to figure this out myself.

"Kiss me now and *say*." He reached over and took my chin and pulled my face to him. I did what I had always done, nodded yes. And I let his mouth come onto mine, but this time for the first time I tasted the spit on his lips. And my mind that was crying out like a crow's caw, "no, no," started to get cunning and to shift around for a way to get Baby and me away from there.

When he'd actually showed me the overalls, picked up the roll of clothes that he'd had in the car all the time and brought out a pair of overalls I'd seen him wear all summer, I couldn't take it in. The overalls I had washed, scrubbed with lye soap that Georgeanna had made with me, standing right there helping her under the shed with the meat grease and lye and her talking about what lye had done to many a Negro's face, had boiled in the black pot to get tobacco gum out of, had starched and ironed, my back hurting, wondering with a mixture of fear and thrill if I was going to have a baby, and if it was Jack's or Aaron's. By the time I'd ironed them again, I was wearing the rag between my legs, feeling both relief and sorrow as I did every single month . . . There they were with a big dark stain across the front, a big dark blot.

For some reason I saw a picture in my mind of strong black women walking straight and proud with baskets of laundry, fresh and clean, balanced on their heads, their clean but ragged children running around their feet, while on a porch a series of men lay drunk.

When I first started to feel a little strength come to me, it was so small, so tiny, it was just barely there. It was as little as a tobacco seed. And that's the littlest seed there is, even littler than a mustard seed. I used to hear Daddy and Georgeanna talk about that and what it says in the Bible about faith, having faith only as big as a mustard seed . . .

Daddy said a tobacco farmer had to have that kind
of faith to stake his whole survival on those little
seeds he put out in some dirt and to break his back
with that blind faith for a whole long year of work
from morning to night.

That feeling was in me, and even though it was
small, it was throbbing like a little voice saying to
me: "I'm worth something. It's too late for Aaron,
he's dead, but I'm alive, and so is Baby."

I looked across at Jack, and he looked different.
His mouth, that mouth that had excited me all
summer, looked narrow and hard, and all over he
was lean and spare, but just a man, just a lean,
spare man, sitting there looking across the room
from me. I felt the seed growing in me. Felt it
plainer than the seed that had turned out to be
Baby, and I realized that the seed was a self
growing. I'd never had a self before, and now I had
found it here in a tourist camp in Georgia.

It was as if Georgeanna came walking in the door
from behind one of those little outbuildings, using
that old stick she used to use when she poked
around in the leaves and trash looking for something, some catalogue page, some throw-away out-
of-town newspaper to read, always looking. I'd
even seen her hold up cured tobacco leaves like she
was trying to read their parchment, never satisfied.
Now it was as if she took that stick and jabbed it
into my side to make me do something. "Move,
Roxy, do something, before it's too late."

Jack mumbled that he'd be back directly. I saw that he was wearing a suit. He looked like somebody I'd never seen before, like seeing somebody clean-shaven when you've always seen them with a beard. I got up and dressed quickly and took Baby, who was bright as a saucer by then, and we went out to see if we could find the tourist-camp woman. I could see her out behind the cabin with the red plaster chickens on the front. Rhode Island Reds ran around near her, and when a fat hen started cackling about laying an egg, it tickled Baby and she started making cackling noises and clapping her hands. I loved to see her laugh, and I got tickled too, and the woman stopped sweeping and gave a dry laugh herself. I nodded to the woman, who said her name was Molly Pond. I knew that if Ruth had been there she would have commented on the fact that the woman's nose sloped down in the front. Ruth would have said, "Well, I see she brought her nose on out in the yard with her, or has she been making pickles?" Ruth always commented on things like that. Sometimes it was funny and sometimes it wasn't.

I nodded to her and started to ask if she had some writing paper. I guess I was thinking that I'd write to Daddy and tell him where we were and see if she'd mail it, but as I started to talk, I saw out of the corner of my eye that Baby was almost stepping in a little pile of chicken mess, and I felt I had to grab her. There is nothing harder to wash off than dried chicken mess that's between the toes.

By the time I had grabbed her up and swung her around, hugging her close, the woman had taken a liking to us, I could tell, so, with Georgeanna poking at me again, I just blurted out, "I need to talk to somebody. I think something has happened to my husband." Well, she thought Jack was my husband, of course, but I told her, I told her all about it and that I needed to do something.

She looked at me right sharp, and while she was thinking about what I had said, standing there nodding, she suddenly jerked out her arm and reached down and grabbed up a pullet that was passing by, and before I knew what was happening she had wrung its neck and it was squawking and flopping long-necked all over the ground.

As Baby and I stood there, watching the motions in fascination, I heard Jack drive up. He couldn't see us because we were behind the house near the chicken yard. I looked at the woman hard and went on back to our cabin. Jack said, "Where you been?" and I said, "I've been to hunt Baby. She wandered off down by the chicken yard." I bent down and rubbed some spit on the mosquito bites that had turned into sores on her legs so that he couldn't see my face, but he must have thought I looked funny anyway because he said, "You told somebody, didn't you?" I tried to deny that, but he didn't believe me.

He started pacing around. "I'm going," he said. "Going now. I've got the bus tickets to Birmingham. Come on, Roxy, I know somebody out there we can stay with."

He walked inside the cabin and started gathering up his things. His eyes darted around. "I've got to go, Roxy, it leaves at eleven o'clock." He paused. "I don't know how come"—he looked over at me, his eyes sick—"I don't know how come I ever thought you'd go with me."

A sob rose up in my throat. I moved quickly, grabbing Baby's hand, and rushed out the screen door, letting it slam behind me. I ran, pushing her in front of me, into the outhouse behind our cabin and latched the wooden latch. We stood in there facing the door, our breaths coming fast, sweaty and trembling. I heard him come and stand outside the door. My eyes were tight and hot, with tears pouring out. Through the blur I could see the little morning-glory vines that were growing in under the floor of the building, growing along the grooves where somebody had cut his initials in the wooden wall. He called out twice, "Roxy, Roxy," low and sad. I didn't look out, though; I didn't trust myself to look into his eyes. Then I heard him moving about, pacing like an animal in a cage, then, "I'll be back, I'll come get you, as soon as I can."

His voice trailed off, and I heard him walk away, hurried now and jerky. I waited for the sound of the car to start, and when I didn't hear it, I knew he'd decided to walk. When Baby and I went outside, the air was a relief. We sat down under a big chainyball tree. In a minute Baby toddled off and came back with a handful of dried corn that had been thrown out for the chickens. We sat there and played with the yellow pieces that looked like jagged teeth. We made patterns in the sand with it, patterns that looked like Indians had been there. It wasn't too long before the sheriff drove up.

Five

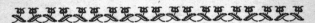

Afterward, they brought me back to town, and Ruth and Gyp took me to Callie's room upstairs in the big old house, without asking questions or really saying anything, and put me and Baby to bed.

The next morning as I was waking up, I heard Callie's footsteps coming down the hall. She tapped on the door with a real soft tap, and I said, "Come in," and she brought me some breakfast that Gyp had fixed. She kept looking down when she came in, and I knew that she didn't know what to say or how to act, and neither did I. I heard the phone ring at the foot of the stairs, and I could hear Ruth talking because Callie had left the door open, but I couldn't really understand what she was saying to Gyp. I heard her say Aaron's name—Aaron Earl Walston, and I remembered in a flash the things that had happened since I had told the woman at the tourist camp and she had called the sheriff.

The sheriff picked up Jack as he was getting on the bus and took him to a jail somewhere near, and Jack had told them everything. Everything, they said; he told everything. That's what they kept telling me, as if they were saying, "There's no reason for you to try to lie, because he has already told us all about everything." Then a sheriff's car came and got me and Baby at the cabin and brought us back to Tarborough, to the police station. I was so confused. After they asked me a lot of questions over and over and I answered them the best I could, they let Daddy take me home. "Material witness" is what they said I was. "Holding her as a material witness." I was so tired by then that when Daddy took my arm, I didn't hardly know who he was.

They told me later that as soon as the sheriff called Tarborough, they all piled into the car and went out and found the grave, drove right to it. In Jack's confession he'd told them where it was, just a few feet from the barn with dirt and leaves over it.

Then the funeral-home boys had to go out there and get the body, and after the coroner and the examiner and all came, they took Aaron to the funeral home.

Daddy and Ruth decided that I didn't have to go to the funeral if I didn't feel up to it. But Daddy said I'd have to go to the funeral home. I had to. I heard him talking to Ruth about it in the other room.

"Remember Sadie Rose Jones that died last year because she got out of the car after the wreck and walked around? Shock. Well, Roxy's like that now. Keep her quiet and warm except when I take her down to the funeral home. She's got to see him or she won't ever believe any of this is true. And she's got to know it so she can live with it somehow."

Daddy drove me up to the side door of the funeral home, and when I started up the steps, going slow to wait for him, I looked over toward the big open-doored garage where the hearses and ambulances were kept. The big new Packard ambulance sat nosed out into the driveway, and for a little flash I could imagine Jack and Neb sitting in it together, smiling and cocky and full of life, reared back pretending to drive like little children do when they sit in cars. I could hear the sounds that children make—Vroom, Vroom, uden uden. And as I watched the two in my mind, the ambulance took off with them in it, Jack driving, Neb excited-looking, the power of the motor taking them away, down a straight road on and on, straight and fast across the town, the tobacco fields, from the piedmont plateau to the coastal plains where the land came to an end in scruffy salted plants, on and on into the foamy white ocean.

Daddy came up beside me and put his hand under my elbow, and we went inside the funeral home. There hadn't been a soul on the porch or outside. My mind went back to one day when I was a little girl.

I had been going home from school and stopped by the funeral home to speak to Daddy about money for some new schoolbooks. When I went in, one of the older funeral-home boys was sitting behind the desk. He blurted out: "We've got your grandpapa in the back."

"We've got your grandpapa in the back." The words didn't make any sense. Why would Papa be down here? When I'd left for school, he'd been sitting by the window tapping his pipe. My hand was in my pocket, about to pull out the Bit-O-Honey I'd stopped by the Little Store and gotten to eat on the walk home, when it hit me what he was saying. We've got your grandpapa in the back. In the back. I couldn't, no way I could imagine Papa in that cold room. No way I could imagine it. Many months later I found the Bit-O-Honey still in my pocket.

There was no way I could make my mind take in that Aaron was in there. But Daddy said, "You've got to see him, Roxy. Got to make yourself look right at him."

When I got inside the front door, the soft rugs on the floor in the hall seemed to pull my feet into them. I walked across the hall and stopped at the piano for a minute. As I stood, I could almost see the notes move and hear the sound of the voices as they sang in a close harmony: "Jesus, Lover of My Soul," and "Rock of Ages, cleft for me, Let me hide myself in Thee." As I turned to walk into the wide room where I knew the casket was on view, the softness of the rug was like a forest and the petals of the flowers in stands around the room waved and brushed by me like little children's hands. I realized that I was seeing in the dust particles of the air that moved in the room, the ghosts of the children that were killed in the school-bus wreck out close to the farm. I stood right by the casket now.

I thought, I never meant for any of this, anything like this to happen, Aaron, but it looks like it was bound to. Like you knew all the time. The way your eyes were always so far away, and those songs you played all the time. I guess it's like those cousins of yours, the ones in that picture hanging upstairs in your folks' house. In the picture they are lying there on the bed dead when they were just six years old, a boy and a girl. Sweet-faced and lost in the woods and eating poisoned berries. They hadn't even been in the world long enough to have a picture taken of them, let alone to learn enough to know which of the berries were poison.

As I looked down to see Aaron's body lying in there like that, I felt a faintness come over me and reached out, hoping that Daddy would be there, that the bigness and warmth of his dark suit would fold around me, hide me. I leaned against him and breathed in the smell of Chesterfields. I automatically put my hand down into his big pocket and felt the white sack lining, like I did when I was a little girl looking for a Saturday nickel. We stood like that for a while as I looked at Aaron, that neat, clean boy lying there like that. Then Daddy pulled me away and led me to a seat in the little room in the back of the hall, a little half room under the stair. I had seen him sit there sometimes to talk privately with salesmen. I saw him and his friend Dempsey there one time, Dempsey with his head in his hands. The rumor was that Dempsey, who delivered cleaning to every house in town, had done something sassy to a little girl. I heard him say that it wasn't true, but I know that he didn't pick up the cleaning anymore.

Daddy said he'd be back in a minute, and after he left I sat staring at the top of the stairs. I saw Neb up there, peering through the banisters like a little boy. Looking at me funny.

It was a look that stunned me. A look that held both fear and a kind of hunger for me. Like an animal lurking. I realized that I had seen the same sly look on the sheriff's face but had been too much in shock to really notice it. I saw it many times at the trial later.

Neb said, the words coming down the steps at me: "You know Jack used to stay up here with me before he went out to the farm."

As I turned to dodge the words, I saw Daddy standing in the shadow watching me, and before he could wipe it away, I saw a touch of the look in his eyes, too.

I went up the stairs; I felt compelled to go. When I got to the top I turned and walked a little way into the room Neb pointed to. The dusty smell was so familiar that I jerked my hand to my mouth. It was just like Jack was standing there. I never knew exactly what the little smell was that was always on him before, but I realized now that it had always been on Jack, the smell of a closed room. A room where the shades were always pulled down and the sunshine never got in. Just stale air breathed over and over. I glanced at Neb. I couldn't believe he slept in there every night. I remembered now that I'd always, time after time, aired out the spare room where Jack stayed at the farm. But no matter how much I'd open it up and air it, he would manage to close it up and get that smell back in it again. I started to feel stifled, and in my mind I could see rows and rows of coffin boxes and children playing in them. I could see myself closed up in one of the two-story ones, the bottom one. Somebody accidentally pushed a piece of furniture up against the opening while I was asleep, and when I woke up panicking, I started to hit the plywood with my fists, pushing and pushing, breathing hard and pushing. And then Georgeanna's voice called out from the distance, "*Push*, Roxy, *push*." And I pushed through to the clean, clear air outside.

I knocked against Neb, shoving him out of the way, went quickly down the stairs and out of the building to the car, then to the house and the kitchen where Ruth and Gyp and Baby waited with good smells from the warm cook-stove.

I went on staying at the house in town. Ruth and Gyp kept Baby downstairs away from me, and I shut the door to Callie's room and just stayed in there and watched the leaves at the top of the trees and listened to the clock at the courthouse. For the first few days that's all I seemed to hear or see.

Callie would tap on the door and leave me a tray outside. Everybody was good to me and didn't try to make me talk about it, even Ruth. In a way, except for Callie and Daddy, who would come and talk a little every afternoon, it was like the way I'd seen people treat people that were dying.

Daddy took me out to the farm once, and I tried to walk around outside, but everywhere I'd walk I'd see Aaron. In the tobacco fields, his voice ringing out Gee-Haw to the mules; on the porch, lifting the dipper to his lips for a cool drink. The cold splattering hurt around my heart sent me away from the direction of the barns, into Daddy's car, back into the room in town.

Once I was in the room, I didn't seem to have much feeling about anything. I kept reading the news that was in the paper, but it was like reading copies of some old detective magazine that Daddy had left lying around. The paper kept calling it a Love-Triangle Slaying and said things like "Young farmer buried alive by wife's lover"; "Body of young Tar County man found in shallow grave."

The trial was set for October 1. It was to be at the state capital in Raleigh.

The day before, Ruth came up and tapped on my door, and the way that she talked and acted to me showed me a side to her that I hadn't seen before.

She brought me a new dress that she had bought at the London Shop. It was soft and pretty. I noticed that my mind didn't jump to think, "Will Jack like it?" If anything there was more of a dreg of, "Would Aaron like it?" But not much of that either.

"Your daddy wanted to buy you one, but I told him I'd like to pick it out. You know, Roxy"—she sat down on the bed, and I didn't pull back like I would have a few months ago—"they may not be holding you any longer, but you're on trial too." She looked over at me and I could tell that she was trying to help me get through this. She saw my bewilderment. I'd been lying on the bed looking out the little window that opened out onto the roof. The white curtains moved gently.

"Everybody that can get there is going to be there—and you're going to have to face them all. Don't worry about Baby, she and Gyp are hitting it off fine. I hate for Callie and Raider to hear some of the things they'll be saying, but they'll be bound to go at least part of the time."

I got up, and she helped me try on the dress, and as we stood in front of the big mirror on the dresser I could see for the first time that though I was a good foot taller than Ruth was, we favored each other some; we were kin. I saw that she really was my own mother's younger sister. And I thought about how I had heard that she had been different—had broken away from the town for a while and gone off to college and graduated, and then life had turned for her when she had come back home and there was her sister's husband, a widower, needing her.

I thought about what I'd overheard her say to Gyp in the hall. "This whole thing never would have happened if I hadn't been so busy lining those curtains for the front room all summer long. I can't *believe* I didn't see it coming, and my own children right in the middle of it!"

Now she was saying, "You just do what you have to do, Roxy. Life's full of little crooks and corners. You never know which way you're going to be pulled next. Nearly everybody in the world's got some kind of secret, but everybody doesn't get found out and have their picture put in the paper."

She stepped back. Putting her hands on her hips, she moved her head from side to side looking at me. Reaching over to tug at the cloth across my back, she said: "We're going to do the best we can, Roxy. Just one thing, when you walk in there tomorrow, stand up straight and hold your shoulders up."

That October day when they put me on the witness stand, I had on the new outfit Ruth had bought for me. It was silk shantung and had little maple leaves all over the skirt. She sprayed some toilet water on me that smelled like dry leaves and then fixed my hair in a different way. She pulled it away from my face and pinned it behind each ear with little tortoise-shell hairpins and just let the rest fall down my back. She made me stand real still while she brushed some dry rouge over my cheeks. While I was standing there, I felt just like one of the dead bodies at the funeral home. Sometimes Ruth helped out down there and fixed their hair and put makeup on their faces after Daddy had finished with the embalming.

The whole time we were getting ready, I felt cold and waxy. But something happened to me when we got to the courthouse. It was like Easter Sunday at church, the crowds pushing to get in the high courthouse building. Except the people had paper-bag lunches and the children were with the dogs at the edges. The reporters from the newspapers and detective magazines called out as our car pulled up to the curb. As their eyes fell on me and the flash bulbs flashed, I felt the coldness leave me. By the time I had gotten into the building, moving under the big black ceiling fans with the mashed June bugs and July flies left over from summer, I'd picked up the high feeling from the onlookers. For a minute I floated in a kind of white haze.

Daddy and Ruth and I walked in fast. People were packed into the rows, and when I came in, there was a lot of motion and mumbling. I didn't look at anybody, just walked fast and straight as I could to the place that Daddy showed us. After we had sat a little while, I glanced around a bit and saw that what Ruth had said was true. Everybody I had ever seen in my life was there and a lot I hadn't. I didn't know how to act, didn't know how people expected me to act. But when I looked up and saw the Walstons led it, they looked so little, Mr. Tatie and Estelle and Aunt Patty, straight and close together, pulled together in a grieving knot, the sight of them brought tears that hadn't come before. A wash of them. I brought my handkerchief up to my face and tried to get control when I felt Mr. Walston lay his hand on my shoulder, strong and warm, as they moved by to sit on the other end of the big bench. I felt worse than I ever had when the big hand touched me. That touch came out of a big hurt that must have been almost unbearable to reach out to reassure me. Out of the corner of my eye I could see my daddy and Mr. Walston sitting there on the bench. It would have seemed a lot more natural to have seen them on the bleachers at a ball game.

The room was full, and I could hear people rattling paper and sticking the lunch bags they'd brought under the seats. They didn't want to leave and take a chance on losing their places.

I kept expecting to see Aaron walk in. I could see him just as plain, sitting at the table that night before he and Jack went outside. Sitting there after he had finished eating his chicken, eating a plate of tomatoes like he always did, spreading them out on his plate and putting salt and pepper and then vinegar over them—looking just as regular and ordinary as anybody else, not like somebody about to be dead. I had always thought about dead people with awe, like they were somebody famous. I couldn't think of Aaron like that, and it seemed

funny for all of us to be here like this without him
being here too.

Suddenly I saw some people come in that I
figured must be Jack's folks. Ruth leaned over and
scratched at my skirt to signal me, and then I knew
for sure it was. A kind of deep shame went over me
when I looked at the poor old couple. They seemed
as old as Georgeanna, and they looked pitiful and
out of place. I thought that probably they had never
been out of south Georgia before. I looked at the
woman who must have been Jack's mother. She had
coarse white hair with streaks still of carroty red.
The eyes that were so sharp in Jack's face were
filmed over in his father's. I was ashamed of
thinking it, but everything about them looked
soured, and I couldn't imagine living around them.

I realized then that they were bringing Jack in
and started bracing myself to see him. I thought I
was ready, but I was still startled when they led
him in. He looked right straight at me, and when he
did every person in the courtroom followed his eyes.
His power over me was gone, and I didn't aim to get
back under his spell, but there was something going
through the air when he looked out at me. I could
feel it like an electric shock, and I could see by the
way they sucked in their breath that the people
sitting out there did too.

Then suddenly my name was called. My knees
wobbled, but when the man took me to sit in the
straight chair up near the judge I tried to walk
strong and proud. Seated, I spread out my fingers
to straighten my dress.

The man they called the solicitor spoke. "You are Mrs. Roxanna Walston?"

"Yes, sir."

"How old are you?"

"I am twenty."

I heard my voice answering question after question—where I'd gone to school, how long I'd been married to Aaron, where we lived and things like that. Then he started about how I got to know Jack and all. He was patient and talked nicely to me. When he got to the part about me and Jack and the nights at the barn, I could hear the people shuffling around in their seats, still sucking in their breath. I told the truth as near as I could, but I would get mixed up sometimes. It seemed like I had already told the story over and over since they first started asking me about it in Georgia, when they'd picked me up.

The men on the jury kept their eyes right on me every minute. I'd watched them walk in and sit down and wondered where they'd come from. I'd never seen any of them before, but I guess they were from up around Raleigh or farther off in Tar County. The way they sat, long-faced as preachers riding mules, I could tell they were trying hard not to give away their feelings in their faces. But I could tell the ones that were blaming me the most. I wondered if it would have been any different if there'd been any women in the jury box. Probably even worse, I thought. Would the air have been full of looks saying *if you'd been decent none of this would have happened*? I just didn't know and anyway, there were just the twelve men. Sitting there condemning me with their gleaming eyes. One man in the back row, the one who had a little bitty head that didn't seem to fit the long body it sat on, kept swallowing every time I answered a question. The way his Adam's apple moved up and down, it was like he was trying to swallow his dinner and it wouldn't quite go down.

When the solicitor asked me about what happened at the tourist camp, he said, "What conversation did you have with him at this time—what did he say and what did you say?"

I said, "I told him I had to go home, and he said, 'You won't want to go home if you see what is on my overalls.'"

The solicitor asked, "Was there something on his overalls and if so, where?"

I answered, "There was a spot of blood on the chest."

They brought out the overalls and called them Exhibit C, and the solicitor made me tell how Jack had told me what he had done and how I felt.

They had four people that knew me to come up and testify about my character. One was the superintendent of the school. I didn't really know him, but he said I always had a good character when I went to school.

When Mr. Hodges, the lawyer for Jack, started asking me questions, it was really different. Everything he asked me, although he asked a lot of the same questions the other man had, was like he was making fun of me or trying to mix me up or make me say something I didn't want to say. He kept calling me Mrs. Ruffin and I'd say, "No, I'm Mrs. Walston."

The paper the next day said, "As Ruffin, nattily dressed in a brown suit, kept his eyes riveted to the witness stand, Hodges got from Mrs. Walston the statement that she thought Ruffin was in love with her. She said she didn't think that her husband was aware of the love affair. When Hodges asked her if she cared for Ruffin, she said, 'I had a feeling for him.' He asked, 'What kind of feeling?' "

The paper said I sat for a while before I answered. "Well, I thought I cared something about him," I said. "I never cared a whole lot." I meant I wasn't sure that you'd call that wild pulling feeling that was between me and Jack *love*.

The lawyer wouldn't accept that. "How much did you care, Mrs. Ruffin?" he demanded.

"I'm Mrs. Walston," I said.

The paper read: " 'I had a feeling,' she said. 'I became infatuated with him.' "

"Do you remember the first occasion you had intercourse with him?"

I thought, *What a strange thing to be saying right out loud.*

"Yes, in the garden while my husband had gone off."

"And when was the next time?"

"I don't know. It could have been the next day."

Hodges asked if the relations didn't occur nearly every day after that.

"Sometimes I was sick."

"But when your husband was gone and you weren't sick, it happened every day, didn't it?"

"Yes," I said.

It all sounded so different when I heard the words come out of my mouth there in front of everybody, everybody I knew and both our folks and everything. That man asked me questions for two long hours and then they read the confession. In the confession, Jack said all kinds of things:

"I stayed home all day Saturday and Sunday while the Walstons were gone. I dug the grave on Saturday about three o'clock in the afternoon. I used a shovel which I got from Walston's house. I left the shovel at the hole. I hit him in the back of the head with my rifle. Knocked him out the first lick. He was lying down on his face when I hit him the second time. I had been sleeping with her—no use to say I love her and will die loving her. I had intercourse with her from June. In a way she knew I killed him and in a way she didn't.

"I have told everything in this statement I want to tell. I know I am free to tell anything I want to tell or not tell anything."

Everything got worse and worse. While the confession was being read, I saw Jack's mother, who had sat stone-faced up to now, press her hands over her ears.

After people testified about the blood on the

overalls and the dirt piled on Aaron suffocating him
and other things like that, the state rested its case.

The other lawyer with Mr. Hodges got up then
and talked to the jury, calling me a "faithless
woman." "After a comparatively short time," he
said, "this man was staying in the house with more
freedom than the woman's husband. She has been
unfaithful to her child, unfaithful to her husband
and unfaithful to her God." He talked on for half an
hour: "Try to bring into focus the picture painted by
a tainted woman wending her merry way into the
path of doom." He contended, the newspaper said
the next day, "that Mrs. Walston was aware 'all the
time' that Ruffin had killed her husband."

Then the special prosecuting attorney got up and
talked. He called the murder "the most hideous
example of the premeditated killing of one human
being by another human being" that he had heard of
in more than twenty years of law practice.

The solicitor spoke next. Pointing at me, he said,
"She is an innocent young girl who graduated from
a little country school and was seduced by this
monster. Not in the annals of the history of North
Carolina has there been a crime that compares in
brutality with this one. None of us has read any
fiction to compare with this."

Mr. Hodges got up then and pleaded for mercy
for Jack: "For him, for the state, and for everybody
else, for God's sake, don't turn him loose, but a life
sentence in prison would constitute a more severe
punishment than the death penalty." He pointed his

finger right straight at me and shouted, "Whatever damnation comes out of this case—she is the foundation for it." When he said that, every last bit of blood seemed to go out of my body, and the courtroom turned black. I felt Daddy lead me out.

I woke up the next day in Ruth and Daddy's room on Robert E. Lee Street. All the way back from Raleigh, Ruth sat in the back seat as I lay with my head in her lap. The trial had lasted for two days and had been over except for the verdict and the sentencing when we'd left.

Radios were on all over the house. Even though we knew what the judge and jury were bound to say, we had to hear it when it actually happened. Whether we wanted to or not. According to Kent Harris, the main radio announcer at WGTM, the jury went out at 11:25. At 12:05 they were back in. The verdict was guilty. Guilty of murder in the first degree. With no recommendation for mercy. Kent Harris said that when the verdict was read to a packed, hushed courtroom the defendant stared intently at the jurors. "It brought tears to the eyes of many women spectators," he said.

The court was adjourned until two o'clock. When they came back in, Jack made a statement. During the whole trial he hadn't been on the stand; now he said he wanted to speak. The radio reported: "The defendant, in a strong voice that carried to all parts of the courtroom, declared, 'They said yesterday that I do not have a heart. I do have a heart—and there's grief in my heart at the bottom.' Handkerchiefs fluttered. Shortly afterwards the judge solemnly intoned the death sentence."

I stayed in the quiet, dark room for a long time. As I lay in the wide bed with its spiraling posts reaching up to the ceiling, I could hear the flutter of the pigeons on the rooftops of the house. I knew that sound. It was the sound of leaving. When I looked out the long window at the foot of the bed, I felt I was looking down a slanted street where I used to run and run in dreams, on legs that never moved. As I stirred and looked around the room, I felt I was looking at objects through the eyes of a little baby. The knobs on the bed, frames on the wall, were blurred. Trying to focus on the wall plaques that Callie must have made in Sunbeams, I could barely read the words: *Trust and obey. Just for today.*

Higher up on one side of the wall, there was a picture of a little girl with her hair bobbed short like Ruth's in her college pictures. The girl was sitting staring at a bird with her lips pursed up as if she was trying to mock his song.

Over the mantel, on the other side of the room, there was a picture of a madonna with white skin, red lips and dark, silky hair falling over her creamy breast where she holds the baby.

"It's a sort of Baptist madonna," Ruth said as she eased into the room bringing a cold washrag and a wash basin. I guess Ruth knew I'd been crying. She bent and patted my shoulder. I let her. As she held the cold rag against my eyes, she patted me over and over. I felt the pats were saying something she didn't know how to say. Finally she straightened up and started smoothing the counterpane.

"You know," Ruth said, "this was your mother's bed, too. That's why I brought you in here. There's no better medicine in this whole world than lying in your mother's bed. It was *our* mama's bed, too. I lay right here myself when I wasn't much older than you are, talking to Mama. I'd come back from college all mixed up and turned around. But I decided, finally, and I don't know if I decided right or not. I turned away from those books and that big town and came on back here where I belonged, got married and helped your daddy with the business, like everybody seemed to think I should."

Ruth was talking in a soft way, trailing off as if she was talking to herself as much as to me. And her mouth and eyes looked different, too, like she was seeing something or thinking something that I couldn't even imagine. Then she looked right at me, her dark eyes snappy again as they usually were.

"Different things happen to different people, Roxy. Don't think you're the only one something bad ever happened to. What really matters is how you behave after it's over. Mama always said, 'When a thing is over, let it go.'"

Ruth stood up and wiped her hands on her little apron as if they were wet. "Now here's Gyp," she said, "bringing you a cup of hot tea with lemon in it."

I dried off my face with the towel she handed me

and worked up a little bit of a smile. "But I don't have the measles," I said.

"No, but we've got to sweat out what's left of the bad trapped in you. We've got to get you feeling better."

After the tea, she got me up and made me go to the table. Gyp had cooked my favorite: stew beef and sweet potatoes.

"Just go through the motions," Ruth told me. The orangey, thick syrup of the sweet potato coated my tongue and nearly gagged me, but I kept swallowing until it got a little better.

I heard the sound of the front screen door and the thump of Daddy's one-sided walk. He came through the house to the big table in the room that was once a back porch.

"Ready to ride, girl?"

I'd told him, after we'd heard that final, final verdict, that as soon as I could get myself to, I wanted to ride out to the farm.

As we rode, Daddy got to talking. "I don't know how to say this, Roxy, but I want you to know a little about what it was like waiting. They called me late that night, the sheriff and all. You know I'm used to that phone ringing all times of the night."

I knew all right. I could see him take a deep sigh and reach over for his pants, pull them on and head out.

"But this time," he said, "I just didn't know what to think. I mean it had to be somebody crazy or a joker. But it did finally get through to me that they

were saying the sheriff in Georgia had called and
that Aaron was probably dead, and you and Jack
were off somewhere. I called Ruth to come to the
phone and try and make some sense out of it, but
she was just as bad as me at first. Kept asking if I
wanted some aspirin tablets. I said I'd be right
down there, and they said it was no use. But of
course I went. I tried to make myself go by the
funeral home, but I couldn't get to the farm fast
enough. Somehow, I thought you might be there—
or was afraid you were—I don't know which. Even
though they said you were in Georgia, it just didn't
seem possible. When I got there, they had already
gone right to the grave, a sorry hole not any ways
from the barn. Anybody could've found it. What
was the *matter* with that boy Jack? What could he
have been thinking of?"

I thought about Jack as I stared out at the bright
countryside from the car window. Jack had been
thinking of being with me, I expect. Of staying with
me. He'd got like I was at first, I expect, crazy and
sick with nothing real but us brushing ourselves
together like two flint rocks rubbing to make fire.
Nothing real but that sick feeling. His mouth on
me. The tobacco gum sticking us together. I'd
caught him with myself—that part that was like a
witch. I'd caught him, and then I got scared off and
cool, and he'd just got worse when Aaron started
taking me and Baby off, away from him. I guess he
felt like he had to get rid of Aaron so he could have
us.

Daddy's words came over my thoughts:

"What was *I* thinking of? Not to see what all was going on? Not to have stopped you—or *helped* stop you?"

He looked so miserable that I reached over and patted him on the shoulder, saying: "It's all right, Daddy. You couldn't help it."

We were both crying a little, and it took me a few minutes to realize, as I stroked and patted his shoulder, that for the first time it was me trying to comfort him.

He went on talking. "I went back up to the house by myself while they were getting Aaron out. I'd seen and heard enough. I hate to say this to you, Roxy, but I heard Abe, the coroner, say the boy had suffocated—that he wasn't even dead when he'd been thrown in and covered up. They were all out there—the examiner from the hospital, everybody. I went up the back steps of the house, and though I knew they'd already been through everything, I wanted to see for myself."

We'd gotten to the farm by then and he'd stopped the car. He sat and looked down at his hands, staring and staring at the insides of his big hands, at the little circles and whorls like he was fascinated, the way people are when they look in a fireplace and watch the flames, the way some men whittle, a sort of way of thinking things out.

"It was locked up," he said. "I could just see inside the windowpane. It was funny to see your and Baby's things in there all shut up and white-

looking with the moon shining in on them, Georgeanna's old woodstove sitting there in the corner
black as a piece of coal. It was all so shut-up
looking, and you always loved to fling things open."
He stopped talking and sighed.

I forgot then how tired and worn out with it all I
was. I saw I was still expecting way too much from
this big-boned man. No matter how many tanger-
ines he brought at Christmastime, and pieces of
sugar cane he'd walk up with in his hand, I couldn't
keep on hiding from the bad things in the world by
forever riding around with him in my mind; just the
two of us riding around collecting for the burial
association, laughing, talking, stopping at little
country stores for Coca-Colas. There was a side of
me that had urged Jack Ruffin on, and that side
would love to have returned the strange animal
look the men had given me at the trial. But I saw
now that that dark side has to be controlled for
everybody concerned. That feeling that I guess just
about all of us have in us has got to be steered into
something good and strong. I aim to find something.

As we sat there, the radio crackled. The words
came on: *Ruffin sentenced to death in the gas
chamber. While charges have not been filed against
the widow, an investigation is still being made to
determine if she had any previously undisclosed
connection with her husband's slaying.*

Daddy put his big hand over mine and said,
"Forget about that, Roxy. They're through with

you. Jack will be put in the gas chamber, and that
will be the end of it."

"The end of it," I repeated. My voice sounded
strange. "The end of it." And as I spoke, I saw in
my mind the white bird flying up in the woods.

When it got so I could think anything again, I
thought: The part of Jack that's locked up in that
jail in Raleigh has no more to do with me than the
part of Aaron that's buried in the cemetery. The
Jack that I was so wild for all the summer was made
out of something in my own self. Something that
wanted to go and see and do different things. I'd
made up things and put them into that empty place
in him from the first time I saw him walking up to
the funeral home. I'd breathed all the things I'd
wanted into him and thought that that was love.

Daddy patted my knee. "As hard as it is for me to
stand what he's done, I'll go see Jack," he said. "I'll
go every week till it's over, just like he was my own
boy."

When we got out of the car, I saw that I didn't
need to stay there long after all. I had thought I'd
get Daddy to leave me for a while to sit on the steps
and look out across the field. Instead, I walked up
on the little rise and looked down the lane to the
barn for a few minutes, and across the field toward
the railroad tracks. The October wind was whip-
ping my skirt.

The memories—the ghosts of the two men—
seemed to have moved on somewhere. Down the
tracks, maybe, like Rawhead and Bloody Bones? I

went back to the house where Daddy was sitting on the steps.

We opened the back door, and there was my house. Closed up without a bit of good air or October light coming in. It was as neat as a pin, though, and I could tell that Aunt Patty and Estelle had been there. That was all right. It was theirs, the place, the farm. No use having hard feelings toward the farm and the house. There was just a little time that it was mine and Aaron's and Baby's. And that time was gone. We closed the door and locked it behind us.

As we were going down the steps, Daddy said, "You're going to have to leave here for a while, Roxy. It won't do you a bit of good to be around here with everybody looking out the sides of their eyes at you."

I cut in. "Talk to Mr. Tatie about the insurance money and the farm, Daddy. I want him to take it."

"He can look out for the farm till Baby gets grown," Daddy said. "Then she can decide her own self."

"Let's ride on back to town," I said.

As we walked to the car, he pointed at a squirrel picking up a nut. I noticed for the first time how the flesh hung loose on Daddy's big arm. I hadn't noticed before that he was getting old. No matter how much he wanted to, he couldn't keep protecting me, living for me. He was just a man. Just a man like anybody else. I couldn't curl up in his arms and hide like in the picture I saw in the paper of the little girl trying to crawl up onto the lap of the big statue of Abraham Lincoln in Washington, D.C.

But just as we got to the car, something came over me. Daddy saw the look on my face and tried to catch hold of my arm, but I got cagey and wild and pulled away and ran down the lane to the barns, and past them to the place where the hole had been. I had to see it, that place where Jack had dug and dug and thrown Aaron in.

As I stood beside it, looking down at the raked-over Johnson-grass place, pain as quick and sharp as the kind that comes when you catch the ends of your fingers in a slamming screen door hit me in the chest.

Aaron dead. Jack to be dead. I saw them in my mind like they looked that first day I saw them together in March.

No, no, it couldn't be true. I sank to my knees in the dirt, sobbing and swaying. All the words, everything I'd heard meant nothing. Aaron was dead and Jack soon would be, and it was my fault. How could I live? How could I go on living?

I hadn't been in the courtroom when Jack was sentenced, but the words had been there on the radio—the words he said before he heard the sentence: "There's grief in my heart. Grief in my heart at the bottom."

I kept saying them, knowing how he felt. "Grief, grief in my heart at the bottom." Leaning over the covered-over hole, saying those words, I felt Daddy's hand on my shoulders. He pulled me against him. The dirt and tears streaking my face rubbed onto his pants leg.

He held me and rocked me and said, "Sometimes there's only one choice, Roxy, to live or to die. There's been enough dying. You've got to decide to live. It'll take a long, long time—many years, but someday you'll get over it, even though all your life you'll be tending two graves."

I clung to the comfort of his body as he said, "You have to go on living, for yourself and all of us that love you, and 'specially for Baby."

He pulled me all the way up and started walking me around and said, "There's just one thing stronger than death, Roxy, and that's love."

We stayed there in that quiet place with the whippoorwills until it was nearly dark.

On the drive back to town, I kept looking out the window. The leaves had turned on the trees. When we passed the warehouses on the edge of town, I was surprised to see tobacco still in some of them. I had forgotten that sales went on after the excitement of the festival. I could see inside where the shafts of light spread out over the piles of gold leaf. Everything looked orderly and neat, nothing like it had during the festival.

Passing Georgeanna's old house, I realized someone was living in it. Looking hard at the porch and the deep glass of the windows, I thought to myself: I've got to forgive you, house, like I'm forgiving

Mother and Georgeanna and Aaron for dying. It isn't your fault. You're just a house. And the house at the farm, I have to forgive it, too. And the tobacco barns. All old houses, I forgive you. Life being so sad isn't your fault, any more than when things are so good and sweet and happy.

All the farmhouses had the winter look, the clean, spare look they took on when the packhouses were emtpy, all the grading done, and the yards swept. I kept on thinking, and the dream came back to me. It was a dream I had been having all my life. In the dream, I stand at a dirt crossroads, unseen, invisible, looking at a house where people scurry about, sweeping the yard with yardbrooms, scurrying and cleaning, going in and out of the house, the kitchen, the front room, seeing through the walls the way you can in a dream. I see a woman without a face, lying in a bed covered by a big quilt—lying unnoticed, uncared for, alone, unheard, dying.

For the first time I thought I knew what this dream meant.

It was as though I didn't have a face until that day in the tourist camp. I'd been in a little dusty jail inside my own self ever since I'd been born. With Jack I'd only gotten deeper into a black-barred jail. But Georgeanna just wouldn't rest until she saw to it that I was out. It was like that song they'd been playing on the radio all summer.

Said a lady old and gray,
I'm not in this town to stay;

I'm just here to get my baby out of jail.
*Yes, warden, I'm just here to get my baby out of
   jail.*

When we got back into town, it seemed to me
that the buildings had all changed somehow. The
little store. The theater with people walking into it.
Even the funeral home's wide porch. Daddy mentioned for the first time that Milo Batts had died
when he fell and hit his head on the stones in his
walkway. I realized that I hadn't known anything
that was going on in the last two months.

Turning the corner onto Robert E. Lee Street,
Daddy said, "You need to get your driving license,
Roxy."

I nodded. "I'm aiming to."

"After that, I think me and you and Ruth ought
to talk about you getting on the train and heading
up to Fredericksburg for a while. My daddy's sister,
Aunt Katie, runs a boardinghouse right there
beside the tracks."

I looked over at him and covered my mouth with
my hand like I've always done at the thought of
something new. I had a lot to think about. Now that
Georgeanna had got me out of jail, I had to be sure I
never got back in.

I heard Daddy talking about getting on the train,
but I didn't really listen to anything but the sound
of his voice. He'd said those same words to Ruth
last night when I'd heard them arguing out on the
back porch. And I'd heard Ruth's voice, sharp and

straight and alive like Georgeanna's used to be. She was saying:

"You're talking nothing but foolishness, Will. That sounds just *like* something a man would say. That's half her trouble now, listening to nothing but ghost stories all her life and always doing something some man thought she ought to do. How can she go off to Virginia or anywhere else? She needs to learn how to do some things first. Some civilized things. That's the *other* half of her problem."

Daddy was still talking as we rode along, but what I'd heard Ruth say last night was louder in my ears:

"She can stay right here with us for a while and ride it out just the same as we will. She and Baby can learn along with Callie, right here in this house. Then, when she's able and gets good and ready, she can go wherever she chooses."

I couldn't help but smile a little to myself. I could picture her right at that minute saying something like that to Gyp while Gyp stood taking off her big white apron, nodding in agreement. And behind Gyp, Callie. And behind Callie, Baby with her burns all healed.

As we reached the house and drove into the driveway and up under the porte-cochere, I could see that somebody had started a fire in the fireplace. As my eyes looked past the slate on the roof, its color soft as a pigeon's wing, a trail of smoke was going up into the air and on and on into the wide blue North Carolina sky.

Callie and Baby waved as we came up. They sat on the doorstep. Callie was holding Baby's fingers and counting out:

William Trembletoes was a good fisherman.
Catches hens, puts them in pens.
Wire, briar, limberlock. Three geese in a flock . . .

About the Author

LOUISE SHIVERS was born one of ten children in eastern North Carolina. She was educated in the Wilson County Public Schools and at Meredith College in Raleigh.

She now lives with her family in Augusta, Georgia, a mile from Tobacco Road. A member of a writers' group known as "The Six," who studied under the tutelage of author Jean De-Witt Fitz, she has published poetry and short stories. This is her first novel.